Minus One

Minus One

Doris Iarovici

THE UNIVERSITY OF WISCONSIN PRESS

The University of Wisconsin Press
728 State Street, Suite 443
Madison, Wisconsin 53706
uwpress.wisc.edu

Gray's Inn House, 127 Clerkenwell Road
London ECR 5DB, United Kingdom
eurospanbookstore.com

Printed in the United States of America
This book may be available in a digital edition.

Library of Congress Cataloging-in-Publication Data
Names: Iarovici, Doris, author.
Title: Minus one / Doris Iarovici.
Description: Madison, Wisconsin : The University of Wisconsin Press, [2020]
Identifiers: LCCN 2020016436 | ISBN 9780299330040 (paperback)
Subjects: LCGFT: Fiction. | Short stories.
Classification: LCC PS3609.A76 M56 2020 | DDC 813/.6—dc23
LC record available at https://lccn.loc.gov/2020016436

This is a work of fiction. References to real people, events, organizations,
or locales are intended only to provide a sense of authenticity, and are used fictitiously.
All other characters, and all incidents and dialogue, are drawn from the author's
imagination and are not to be construed as real.

For Ariel and Justin, with love

Contents

Minus One

One Way
It Could Happen

Eight in the morning to five in the afternoon, or sometimes later, you see them one after the other, the young mom who can't stop crying, the twenty-year-old hearing voices, some so anxious it takes them three weeks and a ride from a daughter to make it out of their house, plus the skeletal ones with tracks up their arms, the doughy ones with rheumy eyes from too much Jack Daniels, the teens with crosshatched wrists. So it's not like you wouldn't notice in your own house. Not like you don't think about these things every moment of every day, but maybe when you get home you would like to read the Living section of the newspaper: Focus on new recipes for lower-calorie lasagna. Sit in the recliner and have someone else make dinner and bring you a glass of wine, but that's not usually how it goes. How it went.

And of course you did notice, not just last year but all those years ago, the little boy who went from following his dad as if an umbilical cord connected the two of *them* to fighting at school, so the principal called you in. Followed by the even more alarming time of silence, and then the time of slammed doors. You noticed. You spoke up. Eight to five when you say something, people pay attention, either the patients themselves or their families or sometimes Social Services. You speak and faces tilt toward you like the yellow swamp sunflowers along 15-501 swing toward the light, and you scrawl out prescriptions or admission orders or appointment cards and people's lives turn around.

Or sometimes they don't.

At church, in the neighborhood, everyone so supportive. In a town of six thousand, news spreads fast, plus it was your idea to be honest for the newspaper. The flowers and the casseroles, the hugs from people who barely used to nod when you passed one another walking the dogs. But. The others, the overheard snatches of conversation are like shivs through the left side of your ribcage, even the clichés: *A druggie and his mother a psychiatrist! You'd think she'd know how to get him help. Goes to show you never can tell.*

The theories:

Parents worked all the time. Were never there.

Father some hotshot engineering dean over at Duke. Brilliant but no common sense.

Maybe it's the genes. The mother was a wild one herself, in her youth.

If they'd spent more time in church.

Or: *She's so busy with her fancy job that the family slips through the cracks.*

Though of course it wasn't you they meant, not every time. It wasn't you who got called in to school: his father went with the boy's mother.

Surely you must have imagined the other comments: *Not really her son, not biologically. A very messy divorce so what can you expect. People split up without a thought to the kids.*

～

You met Finn as a wide-eyed red-headed four-year old, already freckled, pink with sun, who crawled into his father's arms like a koala and then snapped his head around to catch the kiss his father gave you behind his back right after he introduced you. He was already alert to secrets. You offered up your tube of zinc oxide but he grimaced as if it were excrement and his father brushed it away. The three of you strolled through the farmers market, past the crates of rainbow chard and tiny carrots and fairy-tale eggplant. You offered to buy him a sunflower, heavy with black seeds, had already paid for a plastic cup of fresh-squeezed lemonade, but he refused both, eyes downcast. His dad said, "You want ice cream, honey? Want me to take you to the pool later?"

His parents had been separated a year at that point, with the divorce papers due to finalize any day. He was already big for his age, off the charts, carrying within his cells his mother's propensity for height but his father's stocky build, so that he lumbered in a body that made him oafish as he aged. Made him trip over his own feet. Made other kids shy away because if he shoved them, he inadvertently knocked them down. The tips of buzz-cut fuzz were already at the principal's shoulder in first grade, so she showed no leniency when he brought the keychain army knife to school. He insisted he hadn't threatened anyone or extended the blade. No leniency even when you tried to explain it had belonged to his father's father, who had died the week before. It was your one foray into school, because his father was recovering from the surgery for the slipped disc, and his mother was in Wilmington shooting a short film that was to open the documentary film festival in the spring.

Shooting a film that would screen at some time during the festival.

Shooting a film but her scenes were cut at the last minute; bastard director promised the moon but.

Shooting a car dealership commercial. Which you finally discovered only when the boy fell asleep over his dinner one evening. She had let him stay up so they could watch it air on late-night local television.

In the car on the way home from the principal's office, having been suspended for the rest of the week, he didn't say a word. Six years old and sat like a Buddha, arms crossed, lower jaw jutting, oblivious to your cooing tone, to your promises that somehow you would recover the tiny weapon inscribed on the blade with his grandfather's initials. Which you did, many letters and phone calls later, but by then his mother had procured a signed photo of Ludacris, which he received on the same day, and he tossed the little knife onto the coffee table without a second glance, and there it stayed until the housekeeper set it in a saucer of loose change the following Monday, in which you found it years later when digging for quarters to take on the long drive north to take Evan to camp.

~

Eight to five, you refer people to behavioral therapists, to couples counselors, to learning specialists, and a few weeks later you get typewritten reports that you initial and file and consult as needed. And his father did make an appointment with the child psychiatrist at the university medical center after Finn gave him a black eye by slamming a football directly into his face at close range, then insisting it was his father's fault for standing too close, for trying to wrestle away the ball after the third time he said no throwing in the house. But his mother was running late that day, couldn't find parking, had the younger one too, who was tantruming in the car seat, and afterward rescheduled Finn's appointment with her lover's cousin's wife, an acupuncturist who had gotten certified in marriage and family therapy after her own first divorce, who charged half as much as the university guy, plus could get him in within the next two days.

Finn's baby sister almost never stayed with you. Your husband grumbled that though his ex had been the one to insist on having kids, she had never wanted the burden of actually raising them, but the little girl went everywhere with her mother. You tried to stay out of their loose interpretation of joint custody because it led to arguments. Finn was often deposited at your house with minimal advance planning, even on weeknights or Saturdays when he was scheduled to be with his mom. Other times, she would pick him up for a few hours on a whim, calling that morning to say she missed him terribly, taking him to brunch and a movie right after you had fed him pancakes. By the time he was nine, if you restricted television because he had cursed or flouted a rule, he'd demand to go to his mother's. His father usually said no, but Finn would text his mother and then she'd call, and sometimes it was easier to say yes.

By that time Evan was two: a sweet-tempered, quiet toddler whose dark eyes widened with glee at the sight of his older half brother. In the black moments when you sit by the window before dawn, unable to fall back asleep, you allow a truth into your heart: you cherished the days your household was three and not four. It's like rain slithering down the nape of your neck, that thought. You've dedicated your life to helping people, especially kids, get better. But. Such calm when it was you, your own easy baby, and your husband. Dinner without drama, the taciturn man softening at the babbling child, then Evan nestled in his father's arms, fingers hooked around his father's earlobe as he listened to the seventeenth reading of *Go, Dog. Go!* while you cleared dinner dishes.

Finn will have much more stability now, your friends had said in the beginning, when you all first moved in together. He'll finally have clear rules and consistent consequences. You're a steady person. You and his father will model a loving relationship. But the first time you caught him with alcohol in his room, at age eleven, it ballooned into an argument between you and his dad.

"Where the hell'd you get this?" His dad, normally so reserved, became rapidly enraged dealing with Finn. Shook the fifth of bourbon in the air, inches from Finn's nose. "Tell me this instant! This is not normal for a kid, Finn! You wanna end up in jail? You want *me* to end up in jail?"

You pressed a hand on his arm, whispered, *Calm down*, and he turned on you. *"Calm down?* Calm *down?* No way you'd be so calm if it was *your* kid bringing this into the house!" Which he apologized for later, hours later when he was murmuring to you in the dimmed light of the screened porch, telling you that Finn had pinched the bottle from his mother's house. That Finn claimed the previous weekend he had drained the dregs in her glass and her partner's, over dinner, while the women whooped with laughter at some story his mother told, having gone through almost two bottles of wine. Finn never referred to the other woman as his mom's partner. She had been at his christening, after all: his mother's closest friend.

"Did she not notice? Or did she think it was OK?" your husband murmured.

"Do you think it's true?"

"She drank when we were together, the way people do," he said. His friend Karl had called her a life-of-the-party kind of gal. "There's alcoholism in her family. Her grandfather, the Irish side. Sometimes she worried about her dad." He hung his head, pinched his forehead. "I thought she's happier now. She's getting better acting gigs, recognition. Living with Louise."

Your mouth tightened. "If she's drinking too much, we need to know. We don't want Finn going over there if she can't take care of him. Plus . . ." And you were going to mention the daughter, or he was—surely you both at that moment were thinking about the other child—but a crash interrupted and you spun to find Finn standing over a puddle of golden liquid spreading on the tile kitchen floor, shards of glass tinkling, the remains of what you would later determine was the single malt Scotch.

"What the fuck!" your husband exclaimed.

"Don't move—your feet are bare," you said in the same moment.

"You drink too," Finn said, brow furrowed. "See? This was yours. It's not Mom's fault. She didn't see me take the bottle." And he began to cry. "Don't keep me from going there tomorrow—Aunt Lou got us tickets to the Duke basketball game. Lou is the only one in this family who can get tickets to anything good."

"Missing a basketball game isn't the end of the world," you said, to his dad as much as to Finn. Finn, eyes scrunched, yelled, "That's what you think, because you're boring—boring, boring, boring! Please, Dad. It's against Virginia. Don't make me miss that." Looking right at *you* as he said it, cheeks red. You clasped your hands together to hide their shaking.

Neither parent ever said no to him for very long.

～

On the screened porch at four in the morning where you often sit, the upholstery still holds the scent of his clove-spiced cologne, and it's as if he's walked in again, that afternoon in February when his dad was out of town and you had stayed home because Evan had a fever. Finn, fifteen, home on time from school, hair carefully gelled, face flushed: suddenly shy. You'd glanced up from your medical journal and guessed, "So, are you making plans for Valentine's Day?"

"How'd you know?"

You'd smiled. He'd flicked his tongue across his chapped lips and studied his sneakers. Asked how Evan was feeling. Then: "Can I ask you something?"

"Of course." You wanted to add *honey* but feared it would return the hardness to his jaw.

"Do all girls like flowers, or is it safer to go with a box of candy? Like, if she's an athlete."

"You can't go wrong with either," you'd said, and offered him a twenty, which he tucked in his back pocket with a nod, eyes averted.

"But what if she doesn't want either—like—from *you*? Or, what if . . ." He coughed, went redder, his freckles darkening across his cheeks. Peered at you sideways. "What if she doesn't even like *boys*?"

You watched him carefully. There was so much you wanted to say, but he had never come to you with anything before. He had walked out on so many attempts at conversation, especially if they involved his mother. You kept it light. "Do you have any reason to believe she doesn't?" you asked. He shook his head.

"Well then. Sometimes you gotta take a leap of faith. Go for it."

He nodded, serious, and disappeared to his room. For a week or two after, he whistled in the shower and left a trail of musky scent when he walked by. You wanted to ask but didn't want to embarrass him.

Then in early March, over chocolate chip pancakes one Sunday morning, Evan asked, "Why do girls suck, Mom?"

Finn guffawed, and his dad, grin frozen in confusion, looked from Finn to you and back. You stiffened.

"What kind of a question is that? Where did you hear that expression?" Evan, eight, shrugged. "Did someone say that?" You tried not to glance at Finn. "Girls *don't* suck, Evan, and it's not an expression I want to hear you use about anyone. And only foolish people talk of *all* girls or all people of *any* group being any kind of way."

"Yeah, you better brush up on your politically correct language, dude, or the enforcer's gonna drop the boom on you," Finn chimed in.

"Finn . . ." His dad stretched out the vowel, in warning.

"Girls *do* suck," Finn spat. "Or, you *wish* they would"—another guffaw—"but they won't," and he laughed then, and you scraped back your chair and stood and his dad yelled at him but he had already scooted from the table and out of the house, his dad trailing him and telling him he was not to take the car, he needed to come back and apologize. You could already hear the cough of the motor turning over.

You waited up for him that night. You tried to talk to him but he had gone silent. When you reached for his shoulder, his glare, the defiant tilt of his chin, made your hand drop as if burned. He never let you touch him: he flinched if you rubbed an arm or moved back if you sat too close. When he was younger, he'd scowl if you tried to ruffle his hair. He never snuggled against you on the sofa like Evan did or draped his legs across yours while you watched TV together. When he was younger, he'd press against his dad, and sometimes crawl into his lap, and his dad would stroke his hair or shoulder but soon would say, "Gosh, you've gotten so *big*! Go sit over there." You had heard people say Finn's mother wasn't very maternal, whatever *that* meant. You wondered what those people had to say about you.

You weren't going to tolerate marijuana smoke drifting out of his room, and you were very clear about that. Evan was only nine at that time, but you spoke bluntly to him about his brother's problems. When Finn declared he was moving to his mother's full time, you woke during the night and sat alone on the screened porch, eyes brimming, because you knew *that* wouldn't last long. But you were wrong: he didn't come back the next week, or the next.

It wasn't until the end of the month that the frantic phone call interrupted dinner.

"How could she not tell you they were going out of town?" you yelled at his father. "For two weeks! Up and goes to Bermuda with Louise and her other kid and leaves a teenager who's stoned all the time on his own? What kind of adult is she? After you explained he was coming, talked that night!"

He shrugged, then hung his head. "Anyway, I left her a voice mail saying we should talk. Her return text said she'd taken care of everything and would call soon but was crazy busy right then. It pissed me off."

"So you didn't actually talk."

"She says he'd told her that he had a fight with you. That you didn't want him around. She thought he'd be the perfect house sitter for the dog while they were gone." He sank into the rattan chair. "She thinks we don't give him enough freedom. But really I think she didn't want to miss her trip—she was so thrilled that she isn't too old to model. That the lucrative jobs haven't dried up." The photo spread was for a Japanese car advertisement that featured a family. You saw it months later, Finn's mother leaning against the hood beside a square-jawed, tall, blond man, behind an angelic blond-haired boy, younger than Finn.

The man's arm was wrapped around her waist, and her arms were both draped over the boy's shoulders. Their hair was windswept and she gazed down lovingly at the boy while he and the man both mooned over the car.

She had come home to find her medicine cabinet emptied. Gone: The ancient Xanax from the time of the divorce. A bottle of Louise's migraine pills. Their sleeping pills. The house was a mess: a deep gash in the dining room floor, pale-brown stains in the carpets, a dark ring around the tub. Finn insisted that friends had thrown a party without his knowledge or consent; *they* must have raided the medicine cabinet.

You checked the mirrored cabinet in your own bathroom. The oxycontin your husband never finished after his back surgery was no longer there.

You persuaded them to get him into treatment, but he wouldn't go residential. He insisted he had just been experimenting and there was no proof that he was physiologically dependent.

He seemed better after the three months of once a week treatment, more grounded. Louise convinced him to start attending her church, a progressive, inclusive congregation with a gay minister. His sister was active in the youth group there. You encouraged his father not to sneer when the topic of religion came up, but he couldn't believe his ex attended church now, after all her complaints about Catholicism. Finn said she rarely went.

He had grown to be six two, with muscular arms but a soft belly. He could have played football, but his parents wouldn't allow it. For the next two years, he stayed with you on and off, quiet, distant. One rainy weekend he sat patiently while Evan taught him to play chess, played hour after hour with him. You grilled filet mignon, his favorite, and made mashed potatoes. When he thanked you and ruffled Evan's hair, you beamed, and a small bubble of hope rose inside your ribcage.

Still, you never let him babysit.

He arrived sometimes with tattered copies of his favorite middle-school books for Evan. Then he'd ask for the car keys. Sometimes he'd sit late into the night playing Scrabble, or when you allowed it, video games. But the nicest of evenings might end abruptly with a howl from

Evan that he had cheated, or an eruption between father and son. Worst, it might be a yelp when he pushed Evan, unexpectedly and too roughly, sending him into the corner of a coffee table or a countertop. Evan covered for him, said it had been an accident. This made Finn even angrier.

His senior year, he disappeared for hours, with vague answers about where he was going. Sometimes he'd say, "Why do you care? Isn't it better when I'm not around?" His dad planned evenings at the Bulls stadium for the two of them, bought concert tickets. Sometimes they invited his sister. Evan asked why he couldn't go, which made you cry later when you talked about it with your husband.

You said Finn needed consequences for his behavior. His dad said what was he supposed to do, lock him up? He's been through a lot, both parents said. We've made mistakes, but no one is perfect. He's figuring it out now. His mom wrote him notes, which he left around the house. I'm so proud of you, they said. Believe in yourself. I'm so proud of the man you are becoming.

He applied to a single college, which had the reputation of being a stoner school. You tried to talk to him about opportunities, about casting a wider net.

"Sorry I'm not a genius like Evan," he said with a sneer.

His mother said don't pressure him. Did it matter *where* he went? Just let him get the degree.

The night after his high school graduation, you snapped awake to police knocking on the door at 3:00 a.m.: Finn pulled over for underage drinking. His pinpoint pupils worried you, but you couldn't very well drug test him at the house. He didn't wake until three the next afternoon, and when you asked him what drugs he'd been doing, he said some kids had shared pills, but he didn't know what kind. "I just took half a blue one and a pink," he said, like that might mean something to you.

You asked the usual questions, and he shook his head. He didn't meet your eye.

"Is Dad furious?" he asked after a while.

"He's just really worried about you. We both are," you said.

"Everyone was drunk. It was *graduation*, for Christ's sake! Our last big party together. He's not gonna take away the car, is he?"

You and his dad did suspend driving privileges for two weeks, but his mom needed help shuttling his younger sister, who only had her permit, and in return she let him use her car. Plus otherwise how would he get to his summer job at the mall? She came in person to argue with his dad. "You're always putting him in double-binds," she said. "You expect him to pay for his legal fees and for the ticket himself, but how's he gonna do that without being able to get to work?"

"Doesn't he have any savings? What's happened to all the money I give him, on top of the child support I send you every month?"

"I have to run a household."

"Finn does go through a lot of money," you said. He cut through the living room at just that moment.

"Weren't you ever eighteen?" his mom said, loudly, to you.

Finn acted like he heard neither comment.

～

He was academically dismissed before the end of his second semester of college. You found out three weeks into the summer, when his dad asked when the fall tuition bill was due. He had never signed the waiver for the college to send grades to his parents, and he never let on that he was having trouble. His dad got him a job in a lab at Duke. After two weeks, you learned through Evan that he had said cleaning glassware for minimum wage was for losers. He had stopped going after the third day. He went silent when you asked where he had been going, eight to five, all the other days. Before his dad got home, he'd packed a bag and taken off, to his mom's, you assumed. She didn't immediately respond to texts.

～

Eight to five, you see teens hooked on stuff. You refer families to treatment. You administer drug tests. You come home and watch your husband struggle with insomnia. The insomnia started before, when Finn was still in college. Night after night, he'd leave your bed at three, and if you followed, you would find him reading or checking email on the screened-in porch. He needed air, he'd say. But you knew he texted Finn, even called him sometimes in those predawn hours. That was when he could get Finn to pick up.

He got himself a job as a bouncer at a club in Raleigh, and though it meant his hours were completely out of sync with yours, you were all relieved that he was doing something productive. He signed up for a class at Durham Tech. When he came for dinner, he left printouts of the readmission criteria for his four-year college on the kitchen counter.

You suspected he was doing opiates, but you thought it was still pills. To come to Christmas dinner at your house, you insisted he had to commit to treatment. He never came. His mother called, agitated, because she also hadn't seen him in two days.

They found him at a friend's house just before the new year, already cold, the others slumped but breathing. Two needles for the four of them.

~

Your husband takes his daughter on a week-long trek on the Appalachian Trail after. He offers to take Evan too, but you won't let him miss school.

When you see his ex in your waiting room, you discover she had stayed drunk for three days after the funeral, crazy with grief. Her hair isn't straightened, and it bristles like a halo in the light. Without makeup, she has the same freckles Finn did and a web of fine creases crowds her eyes. Everything's so fucked up, she says. How could it have gone like it did? What did we do wrong? We have to do better. The words tumble out in a heap, the most she's ever said to you, oblivious to the others around you. She stands and embraces you, her breath sweet with acetaldehyde, pressing you to her, sobbing against the top of your head. She is waiting to see your colleague. She fully intends to take care of things. Now.

"It's an illness like any other," you hear yourself saying, "and sometimes it's malignant and there's nothing we can do."

She nods, vigorously. Two fat tears ooze from the corner of her eye.

You go and retch in the staff bathroom. You splash icy water on your face, and gargle with mouthwash, and run ten minutes late to your next patient appointment.

~

Eight to five you explain about genetics, environment, opportunity and its absence. You instill hope.

But when Evan comes to you in his pajamas that night, eyes red, and says, "But if he was sick, Mom, why couldn't he get better?" you gather him in your arms and weep into his soft neck, nestling your brow into his damp hair. "I don't know, honey, I don't know," you say, and he hugs you back, and you rock, holding on to each other, both listening for the click in the lock that will make your family whole.

The Reverse Peregrination
of Daniela Lupu

"And anyway, at eighty-nine what can you expect?" Daniela Lupu shouts in Romanian into the phone. As long as she lies still in the hospital bed, nothing hurts. As long as she doesn't stand. "They say nothing is broken, so."

Over the crackling cellular connection, her granddaughter asks, "But if nothing is broken, why can't you walk?" Her own Romanian, American-accented, lacks the twangy inflections of the South, though she was born and raised in Durham, North Carolina.

"Oh well. Eighty-nine. You can't live forever, honey."

"No, but you should do what can be done. Rotten timing, with Uncle Carol being away."

"Or *good* timing. I hate to bother him." Daniela has relied on her brother far too much in this lifetime. He's entitled to his month in Tuscany.

"I'm driving to New York as soon as I get off work Friday."

"You don't need to do that. You have your own life . . . I know how busy you are in the hospital. I'll be fine."

Adina clicks her tongue. "This outpatient rotation isn't as bad," she says. Better hours, but more boring days: the treadmill of droopy-eyed kids with runny noses and bulging scarlet eardrums; their hand-wringing mothers. The occasional rash that requires true effort, as had this morning's purplish bumps on the pads of a febrile teenager's fingers, on the meat of her palms. Had the girl been hiking in tick-prone areas? Any seizures? Other symptoms? In residency you didn't just ignore information that didn't fit. Such as, why was her grandmother not walking? You didn't just look the other way. You took action.

"I'll try to leave Baltimore before the traffic hits. I need to make sure you're getting the care you need. You called my father, right?"

A pause.

"I hate to worry him. He's so far away—what can he do?" A sigh. "But if I'm not there when he calls Sunday, he'll worry."

Adina grunts. "Well, call him. Or do you want me to?"

"Just tell him next time you speak."

Adina tries without success to keep the bitterness from her voice. "That means *I* have to call *him*, because *he* never calls *me*."

"Oh well, you know how busy he is. Work, and now the baby . . ."

"Oh yeah, busy." Even before the baby, *years* before, Mihai rarely called Adina. It's different in Romania, harder, he once explained. She had wanted to ask *How, what makes it harder when you have a cell phone same as us*, but she had been fifteen at the time and it had only been a year since he had moved back to Romania. It was still the time of trying to avoid upsetting or criticizing him, the time of hoping something she did or didn't do might bring him back to her.

"I just wish you'd asked someone else to change that lightbulb," she mumbles now, and has to repeat it, shouting to be heard, mortified at the rage shaking her voice. Adds, "That's why you have a super. I don't understand why you had to get up on a chair."

"I'm sorry; I'm so sorry," Daniela Lupu says. Her voice trembles with shame. "I hate to be a burden." It's been her abiding fear her whole life.

In the windowless residents' lounge in the Harriet Lane clinic building, Adina ducks her head so the intern typing notes across from her won't see her abrupt tears. "Oh, Granny. You are *not* a burden," she says.

~

Daniela had been reluctant to immigrate, but what was she to do when the choice was go to the U.S. with Mihai, only twenty-three at the time, or remain alone in Bucharest? Oh, she had friends in Bucharest, of course, and a secure job because she actually knew quite a bit of chemistry, had excelled in her doctorate, unlike Ceaucescu's wife, who, with her fake degrees, ran the institute. She had tried to stay uninvolved, under the Party's radar. Her late husband had been a staunch supporter, which should have helped their son. When Mihai decided to try his fortunes in the West, where Daniela's brother had moved with his family a decade earlier, she feared the party would try to stop him. Stop them both.

No one seemed to care, though.

Who knew she'd grow to love the red-brick buildings with their ugly iron fire escapes, set so close together as to block out the sky? Who knew that at midlife—well past it really, fifty-five in the beginning!— she had yet to earn not one but *three* patents, to actually make progress in this new country, to do work that affected others? She was terribly underpaid, of course, again working for people who knew much less than she, but what could you expect starting over that late? She was not a complainer. She just did her work each day. She didn't need fancy clothes or trinkets. She put every extra dollar in the bank for her son.

What a lark it had all been! She had learned English, seen at least four states. Bought her own apartment in Rego Park. It wasn't as large or sunny as the one she had left in Bucharest, the one her husband's connections had helped procure, the one furnished with heavy mahogany bookcases floor to ceiling, with handmade leather furniture, with French doors opening to a flower-clad terrace. But the modest Queens apartment was hers. If she ever sold, she wouldn't owe her profits to the government. And she managed to adorn her one-bedroom home with what little she had been able to smuggle out: a couple of her smallest Gallé vases, a few pieces of Dresden china.

And in the end *things* didn't matter; people did. As she had said again and again to Mihai.

It had been so hard on her Mihai. She thinks of him as he had been: Tall, well proportioned, the sandy hair, the flashing green eyes. The self-assured squint on the plane coming over, taking in everything. The slight pout. Ready to conquer. Never one to let any self-important New Yorkers act like he was less than.

He had been so lonely at the start. Calling himself Mike made little difference. Imagine showing up in New York City, with all its opportunity and glass-walled offices in the sky. The discos famous the world over. The millionaires and actresses and even ordinary women, *willing*, the sexual mores so different here . . . and knowing no one. Not a single person his age. No invitations or even interest in his overtures. Not much help from his uncle Carol, other than OK, the place to stay in the beginning and a few half-hearted phone calls for work, and those went nowhere.

Who could blame Mihai for acting rashly?

⌒

Adina doesn't expect him to pick up, so why the sinking thump of disappointment? She tries to sound cheery in the message, to avoid alarming him—"Granny fell but it's not serious; they're keeping her in the hospital at least a few days. I'm headed there tomorrow." What is he doing at this moment? Early afternoon in Romania. She's not supposed to know that he was laid off from yet another job last month, but her mother still gets regular dispatches from the Romanian grapevine. A friend of a friend heard.

She has not met her half sister. She last saw Mihai two weeks into her internship, when she had taken on an extra night of someone else's overnight duty in exchange for a last-minute evening off, so she could meet her father and his girlfriend for dinner. She had had just a day's notice when they decided to pass through Baltimore en route to Disneyland. Change of plans, since they had intended to spend the week visiting Daniela in New York but it dragged. Over dinner Rodica, five years Adina's senior, olive-skinned, dark-eyed, hair the blue-black of crow's feathers, caressed Mihai's arm where it lay on the table. Hypnotically twirled the bristling hairs with her fingertips. When her ice cream sundae arrived, she licked the spoon empty and kept playing it with her tongue, slowly, suggestively, until Adina felt the frozen metallic tang as if it were stuck to the papillae in her own mouth.

Couldn't think when Rodica abruptly asked her, "So, do you want to have children? Or is it only working with them professionally that interests you?"

Adina had choked on her water. No, she made herself say, she *did* someday want children of her own. And then, because the other woman appeared to be waiting, because the etiquette of social banter demanded it, she added, "Do *you* want children?"

Rodica bounced in her seat. "Sure. A little blonde girl with big blue eyes!" She patted Mihai's hand, threw him a flirtatious glance, then giggled like a child.

Adina's own blue eyes widened. Heat washed across her neck as she pulled her golden hair into a ponytail.

Two years shy of sixty at that dinner, her father smirked. Shook his head with an indulgent expression, as if to say, "What can I do?" Extra folds of flesh under his throat trembled like Jell-O.

～

On Friday Adina navigates the maze of dun-tiled corridors in the crumbling community hospital, whose recent affiliation with a major New York teaching hospital serves more to reassure its elderly clientele than to draw skilled staff. Her grandmother sits hunched in bed: the grandmother who three months earlier speed-walked down the sidewalks of Queens Boulevard in preparation for Adina's last visit, walking from the Armenian shop that sold the feta she liked to the Russians who sold the best salmon roe, then to the Hungarians for Dobos torte. Daniela stares at a television tuned to the U.S. Open. She hasn't colored her hair since the last time they met, or apparently even brushed it today. Her dental bridge in a dish on the side table, her lips pucker ominously.

When did she transform into a little old lady like the wizened bird-boned women Adina has cared for in her medical training? Her grandmother's eyes shift. She registers Adina. A sunburst of delight resurrects the old Dani. Adina recalls soft hands cupped around her small ones, teaching her to knit; the animated voice, reading stories to her at night. Later, the gifts of microscopes; afternoons squinting at the moving monochrome universes in drops of pond water, heads bent in unison, knees touching. The birthday cards, the holiday cards that always arrived stuffed with cash.

Thirty minutes pass before Adina is able to roust any medical staff. The doctor, a tousled Pakistani man who is a senior resident farmed out by the teaching hospital, arrives glancing at his watch. No, they haven't done an MRI. OK, could be an occult break in the head of the femur, or maybe the pubic ramus, but they didn't see any indication on the X-rays. She seemed to weight-bear OK. Oh really, she had been walking normally before? She seems so frail. They haven't had PT in yet. He begins to stammer as he answers Adina. He rakes fingers through his hair and tucks in his scrubs. He orders more tests, but they'll have to wait for the MRI.

Adina does her own exam once she is alone with Daniela. It's true that she can stand without wincing, but she can't seem to take a step. Can't, won't: hard to say.

"It's just my time," Daniela says with a shrug, sinking back against the pillows.

"That's ridiculous." Adina again dials Mihai, ignoring her grandmother's protest that it's the middle of the night in Romania.

He doesn't pick up. She calls her mother in North Carolina.

"Poor Dani! How does she look?" Her mother's voice cracks. "I could take a week off from work."

Daniela is emphatically shaking her head. "No. No. Absolutely not . . . I don't want to disturb your mother. She has her own troubles, living there all alone . . . I am *not* her responsibility. Please."

"Let's wait another couple of days before you make that decision," Adina says into the phone. She drops her voice and twists away from her grandmother, slipping out into the hall. "I can stay through Monday. I was going to take next Friday off anyway for my birthday, but I don't have big plans. I'll just switch the days."

"Isn't George taking you out?"

"Mom, we've only been on three dates so far. No expectations."

"Does he know it's your birthday?"

She sighs. She's so sick of online dating. There was definitely a spark with George, however, and this makes her stomach tight with—what?

Excitement? Terror? "I was going to tell him tonight, but I had to cancel."

"Tell him. He will want to take you out. Trust me. Let me be the one to deal with Granny."

Not necessary, Adina repeats. Not yet. "Look, let her son do the right thing. For once in his life, let Dad think of someone other than himself." She squares her shoulders. "But Mom. Thanks," she adds.

A stainless-steel trolley loaded with dinner trays hulks in the middle of the hall. Adina spirits a platter back to Dani, emulating the cheer the nurses sometimes put on as they present the wilted garden salads, the bricks of macaroni and cheese.

Daniela waves the food away. Sighs. Swivels her attention back to the television. She has become uncharacteristically silent, lips pressed together, nostrils wide. People think an old crone is about to kick the bucket and they come out of the woodwork. Hasn't she given and given, enough for this lifetime? She had put half of her own savings into the house Mihai built in North Carolina, a mansion he designed from the ground up, marble foyer, twin columns like a Greek temple, in-ground pool tiled with Italian porcelain. Of course he had planned a room just for her, but why would she leave the city, with its free summer concerts and its movie retrospectives? Why leave a place where she could go anywhere on her own, for someplace where she'd be crippled without a car? In North Carolina, she'd be one more bothersome mouth to feed, an imposition like her old spinster aunt had been during her own childhood in Iasi.

And who lives in that North Carolina mansion now? His ex-wife, that's who. While Mihai had to start from scratch back in Romania. At his age.

～

Saturday afternoon, the doctor reports the MRI shows no hip fracture, but it's possible there's a slight hairline crack in the pelvic bone, as they had discussed. Seems stable, and they wouldn't do anything different anyway: bed rest, then physical therapy. But she will probably need an extended stay at a rehab facility.

"Gran, I'd like to run the films by the radiologists and ortho guys at Hopkins," she says. "Or ask them to recommend people in New York and take you for a second opinion. OK?"

Dani shakes her head. "Thank you, honey, but it's pointless to go to all that trouble. The doctors here are fine. I'm eighty-nine; enough already. Time for me to stop wasting money. Of no use to anyone."

Adina shudders. For an instant, she pictures her grandmother somehow intentionally throwing herself off the stepladder, then shakes the image from her crazy head. "*Use* has nothing to do with it." She squeezes the thin dry hand in her own. "What do you think you are, an old jalopy? A—a dishwasher?" Trying to joke, to summon to mind the most useful things in life. Drawing a blank. Dani smiles a little, though. Dani, who'd make her laugh out loud with her clever turns of phrase, now says, "More than anything, I've always wanted be useful. Even as a child."

"Well, *I* want you to get better. To have the best care. Let *me* feel useful. Just think about a second opinion, OK? Run it by Uncle Carol if he calls? We can discuss it again tonight."

~

Saturday afternoon, finally, Mihai calls. Adina pauses in the frozen foods section of the neighborhood grocery. Her basket is half-full: cherries, chocolate-covered almonds, glazed donuts. A pack of Ensure. Anything to entice Dani to eat.

"Mmmhmm . . . mmmhmm," Mihai mumbles, taking in the details Adina provides. Neither surprised, nor upset, nor—*what does she expect?* Finally, voice tight, cautious, he says: "Well. We'll wait and see what happens."

"Wait? For what?" She hears the childish whinny in her voice. "She needs you to come, Dad."

Silence. A sigh. Then: "That's not so easy. There's the baby to consider . . . Rodica works late, you know."

There was a time when his voice was warm and fluid, when it wrapped around her and lulled her to sleep. When he spun her by the arms until she squealed with laughter. When he let her sit beside him in the minivan to school, seat pushed way back for safety, his own seat pushed back to accommodate his belly. His thick arm always pulled her to him for a crushing hug before she spilled out into the drop-off lane. She never threw him a parting glance because she always knew she would see him back home in a few hours.

How did that person become this one? What had she missed? What did she *do*?

Only recently has she wondered where he would go those school days, between jobs, while her mother worked.

"So bring the baby with you," she says, shivering.

A snort. "On a transatlantic flight! You really have no idea. *Raising* a child is not like meeting one for five minutes in your office, you know."

Adina's scalp tingles.

"No, I suppose *raising* a child might also involve sticking around until it becomes an adult," she says, then holds her breath in the ensuing silence. Did he hang up?

No. "I'd love to hear an expert lecture me on how to be a father, but I have to go feed and change my child now," he says, voice icy, and she immediately apologizes. Bites her lip against the automatic rise of tears. He accepts the hospital phone number, promises to call his mother.

∼

"We came here for my son," Daniela tells the wrinkled Chinese lady they've wheeled into the other half of her room. She's not sure how much English the woman understands, but the nods encourage her. The woman wears a brocaded silk top over her hospital gown and her right foot is heavily bandaged. A pink plastic barrette holds her black hair out of her eyes. "But in this life, you need luck. Mihai is so capable, so bright, but he lacked luck. And patience. Always it's been hard for him to work under people, you understand? To take orders. He'd have been much better off running his own company."

The woman nods. Her eyes glint.

"His father was like that too. And hard on Mihai. Critical. But that's how parents were back then, right?" She drives from her mind the brief flash of memory: coming home from work with a headache in the middle of the day, and across the street, almost at the entrance to their building, her husband walking in with a woman, her back to Daniela, her husband's hand cupping the woman's elbow as if it were a baby bird. The two disappeared into the lobby. Daniela's entire body froze, blood draining into her feet. She tottered for an uncertain moment on the street corner, then pivoted and took the tram back to work. Men were just like that; they couldn't help themselves. Plus, what good would come of asking? Or worse, barging in?

"His father never saw the point of immigrating here. And really, why would he? With his position, we didn't have to wait in line for coffee and we were given permission to have a car." She coughs and throws back her shoulders. "After a time here, Mihai felt it would be best to go back home. More opportunities for him there. Of course I asked, *But what does your wife say?* and he said he had no choice." She doesn't tell her roommate his other response, how he spat, *It isn't up to my wife.* She shrugs. "I don't ask what happened . . . I don't mix myself in other people's business.

"Do you have children?"

The woman nods again. Holds up two twiggy fingers. "Number one: California," she says. She gestures out the window. "Number two: Ohio." A thumb jerks in the opposite direction.

"At least closer than Romania!" Dani says, and together they chortle.

～

Adina brings Dani her quilted pink robe and slippers from home. She brings a bouquet of bright yellow sunflowers and purple statice. She arranges a cornucopia of snacks on the tray table. She demonstrates how to work her iPad, but Dani insists it's too hard for her arthritic fingers. Besides, she doesn't use email.

She does smile at the pictures that pop onto the screen at Adina's touch.

"Ah! There she is, the little sweetie!" she cries when she sees her younger granddaughter. Then: "Your father wants to bring me home to Romania," she says, sliding a finger across the screen, jaw dropping at each new image.

"*What?!*"

Adina lurches forward as if it's the iPad that's imparted this piece of news and bumps her knee on the tray table, jostling the sunflowers. Water droplets jump onto the screen and Dani clicks her tongue and dabs at the device with a paper napkin.

"He called a little while ago. He can't take care of me from such a distance, of course. He thinks I should move there."

A block of ice settles into Adina's chest.

"Is that—do *you* want to move?"

"Life isn't only about what one *wants*," Daniela says as she continues to scroll through photos.

Adina wants to grab those thin shoulders and give a little shake.

"But—you have family here! Uncle Carol and Aunt Ana will be back. in a few weeks, and I don't live that far, and—and your house . . ."

"Your father wants to sell the house. An apartment there is much cheaper. He can hire women to help me. Women are cheap there."

In Romanian, Adina reminds herself, it's the same word: woman, wife, housekeeper, helper. *Dani didn't mean . . .*

She suppresses the urge to scream. She tries instead to remember the little she knows about medical care in Eastern Europe. She tries to imagine her grandmother, in this new frail state, navigating a transatlantic flight, as her father called it. Or a move out of her apartment of three decades. A new city, albeit it in the old country.

"I think you shouldn't make any rash decisions," Adina says. "You should talk to your brother. You have a lot of options."

"Options! Pfff, I've never had options," Dani says, closing the conversation with a wave of the hand.

～

Things progress quickly after that. Daniela does talk to Carol, at first long-distance to Tuscany and then as they inch along the corridor in her rehab center the week after his return to New York. Carol guards her right side; Ana her left. By then she can shuffle along with a walker, but her upper body bends forward like a sapling after an ice storm.

"There are home health agencies we can hire," Carol repeats, face drawn.

"That would eat up my entire savings," Dani says. "What would I leave Mihai?"

"Mihai is an adult who can take care of his own affairs," her sister-in-law snaps.

Dani shakes her head. When did Ana become so Westernized? And what does she know about troubled children? Her own have had it so easy, growing up in New York, graduating from good American colleges, marrying Americans. "In the end, he is my son. He is all I have." Her voice trembles.

"You have your granddaughter, Adina," her brother says.

"You have *us*. Our—"

"Adina is a doctor," Dani cuts in. "An American doctor. Look how easily she navigates this world. She will be fine, no matter what." She stops abruptly and drops her voice to a whisper, though they are speaking Romanian. "Did you know he's out of work again? If only he'd lost a little weight . . . there's so much bias against bigger people. If only he'd been luckier in his marriage." She wishes now she hadn't encouraged him, back when he was twenty-six, to go find himself a wife in Romania. But Adina's mother hadn't been a bad girl . . . just unable to give him the support he needed. "To end up all alone."

"*Alone!*" Ana snorts. "He's shacked up with a twenty-something!"

"She's thirty-one. And who knows how long she'll stick around . . . now that she's got the child she wanted, and she's also the one with the job . . . I worry about that boy."

"You should worry about *you* a little more," Ana says, and Dani hisses with impatience. They are such a small family: shouldn't they be more loyal to their only nephew?

"He can't help the way he's made," she says softly. "And after all, *I* made him. Maybe it's my fault. I gave him his genes."

"You didn't give him *all* his genes," her sister-in-law says.

Daniela stops listening.

~

At seven in the evening on a Thursday in October, six hours delayed, Mihai touches down at JFK. Adina, postcall, slouches against a wall, asleep on the floor in baggage claim. She had asked him to come on a Friday, but the weekend fare was higher. Adina didn't argue, *Why do you care; it's Granny paying for the ticket.* She wants so much to not argue.

He presses her to him—gingerly, as if her slender body might snap—and she throws her arms around his neck. Her fatigue, her anger, evaporate. She asks about the flight, about his back, about her sister. His anecdote about her half sister's budding ability to tantrum fills the entire time they await his luggage.

"I've spoken with a realtor," he tells her on the drive to Rego Park while he scrolls through the messages on his phone. "I've missed our appointment this afternoon, but he will understand. There are already two parties interested in the apartment." He cites a price. It's lower than any she's heard from friends buying places in the city, she thinks he'll be glad to know.

"Well, her place is very old," he counters. "She's done nothing to keep it up."

"I don't understand the rush, Daddy," she says. "Why not spend some time on basic renovations? I bet you'd make up that investment in triplicate!"

He snaps his focus from his phone to her. "Why do *you* care?" he asks.

Her pulse races. She squeezes the steering wheel.

"I'm just trying to look out for Granny."

"Yes," he says, sarcastic. "Everyone's always looking out for Granny. Carol and Ana, with their fifty worried phone calls. You. Even your *mother*, all of a sudden. Yet here I am, dropping everything to come and actually *do* it."

"I'm here too!" she says.

He looks out the side window. "Yes. Now you are. I appreciate you getting me."

~

The weekend is a blur. Adina taxis her father to meetings with lawyers, to big box stores for packing materials, to his own appointments. He gets himself power of attorney, starts to sell furniture. He restricts Dani to two large suitcases. Dani insists it's plenty.

"I need nothing now," she says.

She offers Adina her Gallé vases and gives her brother the Dresden coffee set. Adina starts to cry. Dani says, "They're worth a good bit of money, but better you keep them."

"Of course I'm going to keep them," Adina blubbers.

Carol paces back and forth, inspecting the ground, saying nothing.

"Do you have help set up already? Have you furnished the apartment?" Ana asks.

"Mihai has taken care of everything," Dani says.

Mihai says, "I have the basics. I've interviewed one woman, who might be OK, and have another interview set up for when we get there."

"So the help isn't set up yet," Ana murmurs.

"I'm afraid there's nothing in the fridge for lunch," Dani says, eyebrows an inverted V. "You must all be so hungry!"

⁓

When Mihai says he'll get takeout, Adina jumps to accompany him. Dani presses two crumpled twenties into Mihai's hand.

It's a breezy, sunlit day. Adina suggests a little walk, but he's already breathing heavily, says there isn't time. He agrees to take the longer way around to the Thai place, down Queens Boulevard and up Continental.

"Still set on being a pediatrician?" he asks.

"Yes—of course!" She bristles. "Just one year to go!"

"I hear it's the lowest-paying medical field," he says. "Aren't you always complaining about your student loans?"

She shrugs. "I can take a job with loan forgiveness if I have to." She waits for him to ask her how it's going, what she likes and doesn't like. She waits.

The light turns green and they cross again.

"So, I'm seeing a new guy," she says shyly. "It's early, but he's really sweet."

"Another *pediatrician?*" he asks, somehow making the word sound dirty.

"An engineer. But he's also a ceramics artist; he's thinking about leaving his job once he's saved enough and doing the art full time."

Mihai snorts. "Hope he's got a trust fund," he says.

"He's really sweet," she says again. He says nothing.

They're a block from the restaurant when he pauses in front of a jewelry shop. The window displays glitter with diamond rings, gold watches, necklaces, in styles that crowd the pages of department store circulars. No, she says, she doesn't mind going in.

"We just got Cristina's ears pierced three weeks ago," he says. "I've wanted to get her some little earrings. Maybe with her birthstone, or else golden hoops . . ."

They inspect the turning racks of studs. They look in the locked case. The jeweler takes out one, three, six pairs. "What do you think?" Mihai asks Adina. They agree on a pair of tiny gold hoops.

He smiles and rubs his hands together. "OK. So I've taken care of the little girl; now let's take care of the big girl," he says, and Adina's lungs expand and her cheeks color. He walks to a different display, inspects the diamond studs, the drops with Tahitian pearls. Turns over price tags.

"What do you think?" he asks Adina, touching a pair of delicate white gold bars tipped with diamonds.

"They're beautiful," she says softly. She's about to say, *Don't spend too much, though*, when he frowns and lifts the yellow gold version. He holds both up in the air. "But," he says, "would these go better with Rodica's hair?"

And sound squeezes away and the air darkening around her flickers with gold sparks. *Let's take care of the big girl.* Adina coughs, then blindly pats her belt for her silent beeper, rips it into the air, and says, "I'm sorry, I need to go answer a page." She steps into the cacophony of the street. Tears blur her vision as she lurches into the shelter of the bus stop canopy. She forces herself to take big slow breaths through her dripping nose, to expel them slowly through her open mouth. Maybe

Afterlife

After, it became impossible to finish the painting, or the half-dozen sketches I had fiddled with on the plane, in the bus on the way to the cabana—even waking before dawn on our last day to experiment with rubbing charcoal against watercolor paper by moonlight. During that trip, my preoccupation had shifted from still lifes to water: to its rippling movement, its light. I'd also started to paint fish, abstracted: their silvery, irregular textures, their sinusoid leaps. After, I didn't see the point. Whatever had driven my brushes across the canvas in the sun-washed cabana that January, while he was out fishing, had dried up.

People said it was that way with grief: recommended time. Time heals all wounds, my aunt Lily said again and again. I wanted to shake her in response; scream. But how could I when Lily had lived through her own husband's death at forty? On the ship from Rome to New York City, no less. On the *ship*! When she spoke no English! To be left all alone on the ship with two small boys! A cautionary tale I had heard all my life, though cautionary for what? Don't leave home? Don't marry a man who dies? Don't have children? Surely not that, since now these many decades later, one of those two small, fatherless boys owned a wine store in Chelsea and threw Christmas parties on a rented yacht in Fort Lauderdale. So maybe it was an inspirational tale, in fact: look what you could overcome if you just put your mind to it.

Cautionary or inspirational, the stories failed to touch me. Two years on, my painting sat unfinished in the linen closet, face to the wall. I had sold or given away most of my others. I stayed away from galleries, having had to flee one six months earlier when I went to an opening and my heartbeat went rogue. Skipped beats, a twinge of heat up my spine when an almost sexual longing slammed into me as I stood gaping at a stupid landscape. Though he refused to admit it, Matt had preferred representational art. He gamely listened to my explanations of conceptual art, encouraged my attempts at abstraction, but I wondered if he secretly disliked my newest stuff.

Two years on and I wasn't sure what to do with myself. Leafing through my old poetry books no longer got me going. I'd spent a year of Monday evenings talking to the therapist my mother-in-law recommended, a quiet middle-aged woman whose eyes welled while mine remained dry. I'd joined a yoga class, went spinning, had Sunday dinners with my parents.

I couldn't bring myself to visit his too often. Everyone said losing a child was the hardest thing. Harder than.

On their living room wall, his parents still displayed the two oil paintings I had given them years before, even the one that was not a portrait of their son.

That I remained in the same one-bedroom walk-up on Rivington confounded those of my friends who knew about the life insurance settlement. But it didn't prevent my friend Jackie from asking that I house her cousin Josh, who was spending Christmas in the city to be with his hospitalized mother. For a few months now, various friends had been trying to worm their way back into my apartment, or onto my social calendar, but I'd held firm. Jackie wasn't even a close friend: we had worked together years ago as paralegals, back when I would try anything to pay the bills. But she sprang her request on me as we rode the subway back from yet another friend's baby shower, just as a mild irritability laced with longing pricked my usual numbness.

"He needs to be somewhere quiet, no buzz," she pleaded, leaning close to be heard above the clanging.

"No way."

"He needs refuge."

I failed to suppress a snort.

"Really. He is saving every penny, so a hotel is out. Can't be around kids. I offered our place. He needs to be with someone else who understands tragedy."

"An aging parent isn't a tragedy," I said.

Jackie shook her head. "Not that. You remember—I told you. This is *that* cousin." Her eyes bore into me, filled.

I shrugged. My memory had become crap, or maybe she hadn't told me. But before I could plug my earbuds back in, Jackie murmured, "Who lost his wife and daughter."

I shrank against the cool metal of the door and let the train bang my skull against the glass.

"I vaguely remember. Years ago . . ."

"Yes. Three. The tractor trailer collision."

My lungs stiffened. "Is this another of your fix-me-up-with-someone schemes?"

But she rolled her eyes. "I told you he's remarried. Already expecting. Remember? Do you *ever* listen? He just needs a place to crash for a few days, and I thought—you know." She paused. "You have the loss thing in common."

I wanted to say no. I should have said I was going out of town and had subleased my apartment. But it had been a while since I had made any decision more complicated than what to have for breakfast, and next thing I knew Jackie was squeezing my hand, gushing, "You're *such* a good friend!"

~

Two days later, during my twelfth or maybe twentieth game of online Pac-Man, the buzzer blared. I slapped shut my computer. Rearranged my face.

He was taller and thinner than I expected, not squat like Jackie's brothers. He thrust a bouquet of lilacs at me.

"I was surprised to see these in winter," he said. I rummaged for a vase. He added, "I guess in New York, you can get anything. Anytime."

"Not really." I opened the tap, feeling the water temperature against my wrist. Drowning out his other words. With my fingertips, I separated the intertwined blossoms, pinched off a few brown leaves.

"Well. Thanks for letting me crash here."

I nodded toward the futon. He let his duffel slip to the floor.

"I hope you like fragrance," he said with a glance at the lilacs. "And I'm sorry about your husband."

I did not want to get into that, but I heard myself say, "I like it fine. I'm sorry too—about . . . your wife. And . . ."

He rubbed a palm across his buzz-cut hair and down the nape of his neck. "Yeah. It gets better again, though. Right? You take risks again." He sniffed. "You learn you *gotta* take risks." He swung his eyes from his shoes back to me. "What am I saying? You're an artist—you must be all about risks. Right?"

I flipped open my laptop. "I'm sorry, I have work," I said.

"Of course! I won't get in your way. In fact, if you have a spare key, I'll be off to the hospital, and you won't even know I exist."

∼

Once the apartment was again silent, the yellow Pac-Man disc kept spinning and wilting, defeated. Which was strange. By then I was scoring high enough that my fake name routinely topped the leaderboards. When I entered the maze of white dots, hours floated by. I'd never played video games as a kid, had discovered this one sitting with Matt during chemo. He had gotten such a kick out of trying to master the control keys, which differed from the arcade joystick. *Look: my hand-eye coordination is still intact! You try. Aw, is that the best you've got?*

It had become all I did on my computer.

My head ached and I rose to move the lilacs to the kitchen, where I kept the window cracked open. I'd gotten my first art grant based on a series of abstracted flower still lifes I'd painted the year Matt got sick. Back then, I thought that if I flattened the planes—elongated petals, exaggerated stamens—I could extract something special, unique: a new way of seeing. A different kind of beauty. Now I saw that flowers were just flowers, best left alone. Dead in a vase, they would start to change at once, their plumpness going slack, more petals fluttering to the ground each day until you had to get out the broom.

Had Jackie remembered? Had she told Josh that lilacs used to be my favorite?

I sat back down at my computer. My eye snagged on the shirt Josh had changed out of, thrown over the back of the futon. My legs jiggled. Restlessness crawled into my ribcage. The badly ironed button-down still held the shape of him, arms akimbo. I hated that this tightened my throat, but it did. I gave in, rose, shook the shirt, folded. Sniffed. The scent of clove-sandalwood-sweat sent heat slapping into my neck, arms, chest. I dropped the shirt and went to wash my face.

I abruptly had no desire to return to my screen.

I thought about boxing up the row of button-downs that still hung in our closet.

In *my* closet.

Instead, I swallowed half a Xanax, then went to take a nap. And slept through to the next morning, by which time Josh was already gone again.

∼

He had left a half-dozen glazed donuts on the table. I ate two. I booted up my computer with new energy: today I would not waste hours on adolescent games.

Matt had been almost as excited as I was when I first discovered the artist David Hockney's iPad paintings, something he had started making in his seventies. Matt's last gift to me had been an iPad, but I had barely set it up. *Matt would want you to shatter the paralysis and really attempt what you keep telling everyone you are already doing*, I told myself again.

I am ready. Today I will start making art again.

After just one game.

∼

It wasn't until the door opened and I jumped and heard the strangled yelp escape my throat that I had any idea that I was sitting in darkness. I slammed shut my computer. Josh laughed first, then apologized.

"Did I interrupt your work?"

"It's OK."

"You were really engrossed," he said. "Jackie said you're into digital art." He flicked on the lights and eyed my bare walls. "You don't display your stuff?"

"No."

"Anything I would've heard of? Do you exhibit locally?"

I shook my head.

"Must be tough to make a living. What are you working on now?" He took a step toward me, face angled toward my computer, a gleam lighting his eye. "Or was it online porn you were watching?" I clamped my teeth against the blush I could feel splaying across my skin.

"I'm entitled to watch whatever I damn please in my own house."

His laugh turned uncertain as he put up his palms.

"Just kidding—kidding! Man, you're so serious!" He stripped off his jacket and gloves and unzipped his backpack. "My mother's too tired from the chemo to do much today besides sleep and puke." His voice cracked and I bit my upper lip. But then he said, "She insisted I do something fun. Can I take you to dinner?"

"Umm—no, there's no need . . ."

"It's Friday. You're not gonna make me eat alone?"

Tilting his head at me, pouting. Flirting.

Was he flirting?

"Jackie said you're super nice. And look." He slid a bottle of Tito's from his backpack and waggled it in the air. "Happy hour. I can make us vodka tonics, or screwdrivers, or martinis. Depending on what's in your fridge."

I wanted to say, *I thought you were saving every penny,* but I said, "It might have to be shots if you're relying on that," and before I could stop myself I had smoothed down my hair and unrolled the sleeves of my sweatshirt. He went to the kitchen, gave a triumphant "Ah-*hah!*" and returned holding a bottle of vermouth and a jar of olives.

I said, "Those are over two years old. And I don't know where the shaker is."

Humming, measuring nothing, he filled an old plastic take-out container with ice, poured vodka, splashed vermouth. "These will be stirred, not shaken," he said, plunging his index finger theatrically into the mix. "She won't let me drink at home. Just because *she* can't, why do *I* have to suffer?"

"Your mother?"

He snickered, slapped a plate over the soup container, inverted it over two of my water tumblers. Squinted as he poured.

"Not Mom. Erika. My wife. Though it *is* a little hard to tell the difference right now, when all Erika does is sleep and puke too!" Again the brassy laugh. My jaw ached. I took a gulp of martini.

I'll call Jackie, I decided. *She has to come get him. I'll let him get drunk and then call her. Not my problem if he has to take the subway in from Queens. Let her kids keep him up all night.*

"All right, so you're not in the mood for jokes." He cocked his head. "Erika wouldn't mind that I said that, you know. She's a fun girl. She could drink me under the table when she wasn't pregnant."

I hadn't had a drink in months. Now the vodka warmed me, throat to abdomen. My limbs went soft. I hadn't had a martini since Mexico— or had we stuck to margaritas there? The details already were slipping. That last evening, January, the Adirondack chairs facing the Gulf, the pale winking water lapping against the sand: I remembered *that.* The pink seeping into turquoise after the sun disappeared. His descriptions of the tarpon he had landed, his beaming face. And when I had smiled and said, *Everything seems so normal,* he had said, *We're gonna make it through this, Sarah, I promise. I don't intend to die at thirty. You have to think positive, all right, for me?* Thinking positively didn't come naturally to me, but as I nodded, I believed him. I tousled his loose sandy curls and told him about the painting I had started. He wanted to see, but I had turned it toward the wall, wanted to finish it first. He said he would wait. He was glad I was focusing again. *You're always letting something get in the way,* he'd said, squeezing my hands in his.

"Hey! You OK?"

I blinked and it was Josh before me, Josh, not Matt. No smile, for a change. "Look, if I'm bugging you, if I said the wrong thing . . ." Voice softer, lines deepening around his eyes. If his face morphed into the look of pity that I knew way too well, I wouldn't be able to bear it. I downed half my drink.

"I'm fine. Great. So. When did you two meet?" I said in a rush, then shook my head. *Slow down.* When had I become someone who needed to brush up on how to interact with humans? "You and Erika?" I added.

"Two years ago. Married a year next week."

"Wow."

"I know. But she's so fun. She makes *me* fun." He lifted an eyebrow. "You think it was too soon? After?"

"Who am I to judge?" I stood; the room spun. I had forgotten to drink water today. Again.

He grabbed my wrist, eyes dark and flat.

"Listen, I was about as low as any human being can be. I wanted to die."

I chewed my upper lip. Examined his shoes. Twisted my wrist out of his grasp.

"I know how much it sucks, why all you do is work," he continued. "People tried to get me out again, and instead I took off for a while."

This got my attention. He'd gone red and was rubbing his palm across the top of his head. He looked unmoored.

"Anyway—if you don't want to come out to dinner, that's fine. I'm good at meeting people. It's almost Christmas and I won't be the only tourist." And as if he had flipped a switch, his face brightened. "I'll even go dancing by myself if it comes to that. But it'd be more fun to go with you. I'll buy dinner, take you for a spin . . ."

Like some old car? I thought. But already my legs were springs, my skin electric. I felt the pulse of bass within me. That the word "dancing" could still do this quickened my breath. I drained the last drops in my glass.

"I'll need a half hour to shower and change."

"No rush. Have another drink."

"We could grab something quick to eat, like maybe ramen at one of those places." Where we could sit at a counter and it would be too loud to talk.

～

Instead he took me to a white-tablecloth, candle-beside-a-sprig-of-holly type of place at which he had a table waiting. Halfway through our bottle of cabernet, he was telling a story about private ski lessons he had given the twin sons of a hedge fund multimillionaire and, making a point, he tapped the inside of my wrist, then ran his finger up my arm to the crease of my elbow. I shivered, said, "What are you doing?" and laughed, because suddenly I could.

"I'm just carpe-ing the diem, baby," he said, which made me laugh again. "You have a beautiful smile. Shame not to show it off."

No, I told myself. *Flirting with some random guy is* not *what I needed. No. It cannot be that simple or that cliché.*

The wine was velvety and I lingered over my glass, inhaling the fragrance while I held the liquid in my mouth. We used to order by the glass when we went out, because I never drank much. Artists are supposed to, but I didn't. Matt liked wine, and martinis, and aged bourbon. He would talk nonstop, draw words out of me. He was the rock climber, the one who bound his ankles with a huge rubber band and let himself be dropped off a bridge, the optimist. We had been twenty when we met.

I made myself say, "So, Josh, tell me what you do."

"Well . . . I'd been climbing the corporate ladder at Bank of America, I mean—before—and then after . . . I said screw that, and left."

I had never quit a job in my life. Or stood someone up for a date, or smoked a damn cigarette.

"Because life's too short, right? I was only gonna do exactly what made me happy."

At least now you can do what you've always wanted to do, without worrying about money, my best friend, Annie, said, after.

Now you have time and *money*, my mother said.

"So, I guided for a while—canoeing and rafting in the summer, ski lessons in the winter. I met Erika on the slopes." Josh smiled and drained his glass. "She says it was the combo of altitude and alcohol that drove her into my arms. Ha! Did we have fun. Park City in winter, Canada in the spring. Then we just stayed on for the summer tourism season. Totally exploded the old me—it was the only way."

"The old you didn't ski?"

"Well, yeah, but not like that. It was *so* liberating. No obligations, nothing to tie you down . . . just basking in the true beauty of each and every moment." He sighed, refilled his glass, and gazed into it as he twirled it. "As an artist, I'm sure you can appreciate that."

"Yeah, more and more I think I was never an artist," I mumbled.

He frowned. "Really?"

I didn't want to talk about that with him.

"So, now that your mom's sick, here you are. Meeting obligations again. Being good."

"I *am* good. Plus"—he leaned close, his breath skimming warm against my cheek—"I had some job interviews lined up too. Not to move to the city, but to get offers I can play against the ones back home. You know the drill."

I must have looked surprised.

"Erika said one of us has to have a job with health insurance, you know, baby on the way." He snorted. "She doesn't get it. *You* get it, though, right? I mean, I *had* health insurance, money, the house, the car seat we checked like they tell you, and still . . ." He opened his palms like a book, and for a moment I sank into the agony that flashed in his eyes. But he tilted his head back, shot out a breath, and said, "*Whoo!* Are you done eating? Because I am ready to *boo*-gie!"

～

He danced like the Jersey boys I had gone to high school with, beefy football players who hopped up and down and pumped fists in the air. He landed on my toe and didn't register my wince. But when I closed my eyes, the music slid through me and I became a river, an eddy of movement, arms loose and warm, drums pulsing through my arteries, clicking with my heart valves, buoying me. I peeked once just to make sure it was Josh and not some stranger who had moved behind me, pressing against my ass now as the beat changed, and in response to his erection I turned and looped my arms around his neck and shimmied against him, and then his tongue was salty in my mouth and he put one hand on either side of my face and drew me even closer and I would've laughed if I could, because I saw that all the things I had worried about in the past two years, like how I would ever kiss someone again without thinking of Matt's plush lips or worse catheters and antiseptic and death—all these were thoughts that had no place in the moment of kissing when everything is pure sensation, flames zapping my body, mind blank.

～

We didn't speak, but he stroked my palm in the cab, warm fingers sending electrical zings up my arm into my spine, making me go wet. The lights blurred outside the windows, neon reds and indigos of club signs, blaring whites of fast food places, stuttering amber streetlights. The radio blared music in Spanish. The driver darted through traffic with a staccato rhythm that used to make me sick. *Find the glorious empty space behind your skull,* my yoga teacher said on Tuesdays and Thursdays, and I would smirk, but now here it was, blue, white, beautifully vacant. Emptiness in my skull expanding to encompass everything.

I giggled when it was Josh who had to unlock my apartment door, and he laughed too. Sentence shards like *parody of domesticity* and *wouldn't his wife be* fluttered into me and floated out, clear empty balloons, just as my yoga teacher had encouraged. *Observe the thoughts and let them drift free. Begin to practice the art of letting go.*

I fumbled with the lamp on my nightstand as I kicked off my heels, and when I turned, my breath caught because Josh was reading his mobile and his mouth had tightened into a line. When he glanced up, I said, "Carpe diem?" And he tossed the phone onto the unopened stacks of mail on my makeshift desk, which used to be my husband's, but I wasn't thinking of Matt, wasn't thinking, was *exploding* myself.

His hands were so gentle against the vertebrae in the curve of my neck, then my Adam's apple, then circling my nipples . . . so gentle and tentative that I had to be the forceful one, smash my lips against his, grab his back, and right before he arched his neck slightly away from me and murmured, "Do I need a condom, or are you . . . ?" I said, "No, I'm good," though I had stopped taking birth control pills three months before that trip to Mexico, had tried in those last few months everything I had read—timing, lying on my back for thirty minutes after, acupuncture, vitamins—though of course by the time Matt started treatment he was rarely in the mood. I had in fact just started to read up on freezing sperm when.

But I wasn't thinking about Matt. My mind went blank when Josh thrust into me, my body moving forward to receive him, his hands pressing the small of my back so we locked into one warm joyous now, and it took me a moment to recognize the guttural animal noises as rising from my throat. His answering syllable was *yeah*, over and over, and just before I came, I pictured myself as a clear cellophane balloon rising up through my ceiling, lilac-scented, into the star-filled night. As I started shaking, the balloon burst and abruptly I was weeping, silently at first while he kept going, going and going until he came inside me, and by then I was shivering and crying aloud and he pulled away from me and peered down at me in alarm.

"What happened?" he said. "I thought . . ."

I dragged the corner of the sheet across my face. Made myself press against him. Squeezed my eyes shut and tried to find the silent, empty place.

"No, I was having a glorious time," I said.

His breath still fast, ragged, he asked, "Don't tell me you haven't— have you—since . . . ?"

Which I would have preferred to not answer. But I shook my head.

He sighed, slid the blanket over both of us, and wrapped me in his arms. Which felt good, in the way that a hot cup of tea feels good when you have the flu. We lay that way for so long that I thought he had fallen asleep. The room spun every time I closed my eyes. I focused on the still blades of the fan above my bed, then book spines on my night table, then his thin hairless chest, so unfamiliar. After a while he released me, and ran a hand down my arm, then up and across my chest. When I kissed him, our teeth clicked and I tasted blood. When I mounted him, he groaned, "Wow," sounding surprised.

~

While he visited his mother, I went through my stacks of mail, paid bills, threw out fliers and unread magazines. I answered five emails and installed website-blocking software on my computer. I stared at files containing photographs of my old paintings. I showered. I discovered one unused ovulation kit still under my sink, but it was past expiration and I tossed it, then took the plastic bag containing it out to the incinerator.

When we had sex the second night, I asked, "Do you feel guilty?"

He sucked in a deep breath and said, "Now I do." Laughed a tinny, nervous laugh. "Look. This is just something . . . well, we both of us needed it. I was never someone who cheats."

"Me neither."

"Aren't artists free spirits?"

"I guess I wasn't." I waited for him to counter with *You can be anything you want to be.* What everyone else was constantly telling me.

He touched my wrist. "We're just damaged souls."

I swallowed. I wanted to say *We are?* but my teeth had started to chatter even with the radiators hissing. I slid the blankets up to my chin. I wanted to send him back to the futon. He pulled me to him and soon was snoring. I lay awake.

The next day, he flew home.

~

And I'm telling my best friend, Annie, a version of this on Christmas Day as we inch through the Holland Tunnel, telling her even though I had promised myself I would tell no one, telling her though I had spent the night trying to think of anything else. Annie's face opens into the surprised smile that takes me back to ninth grade, when we first met in French class. "Tell me everything! Who is he? How did you meet?"

I watch the grimy tiles slip past the window. We had thought everyone would be where they were going by now, but instead the traffic is bumper to bumper. How many times have we taken this trip, Annie and me, headed home to our parents?

"I don't mean a *romantic experience* romantic experience, exactly," I clarify. "It was weird. But remember. Weird is my normal now."

"I know, sweetie."

If anyone can understand, it's Annie. Annie, who broke off her only engagement six years ago when she decided she couldn't follow her fiancé to the Midwest after all. Annie, who then went through more boyfriends than I could keep track of. Annie, who I've rescued from more than one bar, and not just during college. Annie, who still calls me weekly even when, these last two years, I rarely pick up or return her calls.

So I tell the full version. Words tumble out in a torrent. Annie's smile freezes. Her lips quaver.

After a beat, she says, "Well. If it made you feel better."

I hug myself.

"It did."

"I'm glad."

"You don't look glad."

"I'm focusing on not rear-ending the guy in front of me."

I swallow. "*I'm* not the one who's married. *I* didn't do anything wrong."

Annie, looking straight ahead, blinks. "Guess not."

"We didn't use protection," I say, and Annie slams the brakes and the minivan behind us blares its horn.

"I might have an extra Plan B at my house," Annie says.

"Maybe I'm glad we didn't."

"*What?*"

I turn back to the tiles. Stupid of me to think she might understand. After a few minutes of silence, she says, voice soft, "Is he a nice guy?"

And I have to sigh and say, "Not really."

Annie mutters something under her breath.

"He's been through a lot," I say. "Like me." *Damaged souls.*

"Yeah."

"I've never judged *you.*"

She wriggles in her seat. "No—I'm not judging you, honey! You've just always been so—solid. The woman who remembers everyone's birthday and—remember?—borrowed a car, at *midnight*, to come rescue me and that nut Alphonse when his car broke down on the Triborough Bridge. While it was *hailing.*" She sniffs. "Not the woman who gets pregnant by some other woman's husband who she just randomly hooked up with." She pauses. "You were the one who had her shit together. At *twenty*! And you and Matt were . . . well, an *inspiration.* Cheesy as that sounds. So good together." A tear snakes down her face and my jaw clenches because why the hell is everyone *else* always crying about Matt when *I'm* the one who has to get through the rest of my life without him? Sniffling, Annie says, "Even when it made me crazy jealous to be around you two, you guys were, like, a reminder of what things can be when the stars align and—oh, never mind."

"Matt and I wanted children," I say, as if it makes a difference.

"Oh, sweetie." Annie swats at her glistening cheeks, then reaches a hand blindly toward me. I shrink closer to the door.

The traffic eases as we emerge from the tunnel into the sleet. Annie clicks on the radio.

⁓

"Don't you look pretty!" my mother says, standing in the vestibule. "Annie, doesn't she look pretty? More color in her face, a kind of— liveliness?"

"I look the same," I mumble.

Annie nods and looks at her shoes. "Well, my parents are waiting . . ."

"Don't you want to say hi to Sarah's brothers? And the little ones?"

As a swell of children's voices crests, I bite the inside of my cheek, hard. I used to love seeing my niece and nephews. Annie glances at me and away.

"I'm so late already. . . . say happy Christmas to everyone." When my mom turns away, Annie grabs my hand, squeezes it, leans close. "Didn't mean to bring up Matt. You have every right to forget. Do whatever it takes."

I step into the house. A tsunami of children rolls at me, my sisters-in-law streaming behind, telling them *Stop*, telling them *Give her a second*. I surprise us all by dropping to my knees, coat still on. Arms open, I let them flood me.

⁓

Tucked into my old twin bed that night, I try to match the rhythmic breaths of my seven-year-old niece, asleep on the trundle beneath me. Around us the walls teem with a childhood's worth of my paintings. I still brim with the energy of my nephews and niece: my left knee abraded where the oldest tackled me too exuberantly into the carpet, my side sore from laughing in our tickling contest. They calmed when I read them to sleep; I didn't. For hours I had become, again, their fun-loving aunt. I'm good with kids, have always been. And if I'm not an artist, what is wrong with moving on to other goals? I have, as everyone keeps reminding me, time and money now.

Time and money.

My breath outpaces my niece's. Thoughts spin one into the next. If I'm pregnant, will the child look like Josh? I try to conjure his face. What shade is his hair? Eyes? I'm still slightly sore so I know I didn't imagine the sex. What is the timbre of his voice? I draw a blank. I drop my hands against the hollow of my stomach.

And Matt's face appears, a semaphore behind my eyelids. Not thin like during the final weeks, but full, sprinkled with reddish stubble, the dot on his earlobe where he had let an old piercing close up, the half-moon scar over his left eyebrow where his dad accidentally hooked him while teaching him to fish. The hazel eyes with gold circling the pupils. Matt's gravelly tenor, Matt saying, *Is this really you, hon?* My eyes fly open. When had he last said that to me? Was it when I nearly took that lucrative summer internship at a firm I hated, instead of the unpaid gallery one he knew I wanted? Or just before winning the grant, when I told him maybe it was time to move on, law or business school, like our friends? *Is this really you?* he had said.

And also, *The money will come.*

And the money *did* come.

In the stale heat of my childhood bedroom, I whisper words like a prayer: *Matt. I would've slept on the streets, would've worked for minimum wage for the rest of my life. If it could've changed* this.

I wait for the vision to respond to *that*. But beyond pinpricks of gold in the dark: nothing. My eyeballs ache. He is gone.

I don't want to toss on the creaky mattress and wake my niece. One vertebra at a time, I rise. The old clock radio glows 1:12. I creep back down to the main floor, shivering because my mother dials down the heat at night. The living room is strewn with stuffed animals and our half-built Lego town, with the sheaves of pastel drawings my niece produced. I sink into the shag carpet next to the coffee table but reach past the newspaper lying there to the unlined watercolor pad. I tear out three blank sheets.

"Dear Josh," I write. The paper is silky and thick beneath the gel pen's nib. "I'm wondering if when you first started dealing with your wife's death, you found yourself doing—" but this makes me stand and pace and I ball up the page and discard it directly into the kitchen trash.

I think, *Dear Josh, When we were together did you feel any*—but I close my eyes and shake my head. I don't actually care what he felt. I take three laps around the kitchen, then perch at the breakfast bar.

There had been no breakfast bar, no granite countertops, when I was growing up. Before the remodel, I had had an easel here, where the light poured in. I painted in the afternoons before homework while my mother cooked dinner. I painted full days on the weekends while they all watched football in the next room. I once almost missed a final exam in college because I was touching up my art portfolio for a pass/fail class.

Now, in silky gel ink, I write: "And skin to skin she began to remember colors, and the feel of the water in July in Nag's Head, salt sand sky and there you are casting the line into the surf and there I am."

And I freeze. A hard lump plugs my throat. I cough, swallow. My fingers cramp and I write and words bump against each other, some illegible. And I write. Poem, story, letter to the dead . . . who knows. I pause, the ache at the base of my tongue creeping into the back of my skull, then forward into my eyes, my nose, my whole body, and after a minute I give in and the tears come and come.

When I wake just before dawn, cheeks tight with dried snot and tears, I'm shivering. *Dear Josh*, I think but do not write. *Do some people explode before they intend to—such as, right when they fear they've lost their soul? If so, are there ways to find the pieces that scattered like ash?* Which makes me think of the first lines of a poem, the words opening an ache that stings my eyes and also makes me feel like singing. Instead I find my phone. *Can we drive back tomorrow instead of in two days*, I text Annie. *Unless you know how to get the meds for me here?* I picture the phone flashing unseen in the dark.

In the morning, Annie will get back to me first thing. That's how Annie is.

I tiptoe back into my room and pause at the sight of my niece sprawled on top of her blankets. I want to sink next to the sleeping child, scoop her to me, nestle against the hot crook of her arm, wrap myself around the small snoring body. Make a small snoring body to have for my very own. Instead, with great care I pinch the blankets out from under this girl's ankle and lay them back over her. There's almost enough light now for a quick photo of the way her brown-gold ringlets splay against the blue of her pillowcase, a perfect study for a later painting. My shivering ceases.

Because *that's* really me, I want to say to Matt, to the child, to *anyone*, and all at once it doesn't matter that there's no one there to hear me say it as the sun inches its way into the day.

Plymouth

The knife beats a staccato rhythm against the cutting board, slicing shallots, mincing herbs for the gravy, anchoring Will to the marble countertops of this beach rental for which he's paid a small fortune because it's Thanksgiving and Barb insisted on including not just her friends Tony and Ron but also Brenda. On top of Barb's mother, who you would think might help with the cooking but who has instead stormed off to her room after Will asked her to lay off yelling at their son. He did not raise his voice, and even counted to twenty before he said a thing, but still her lips pulled into a purse-string knot and that was that. Nor was she exactly wrong: Aidan, three, has resumed streaking around the kitchen, belting out the *Spiderman* theme song at full volume, bumping his outstretched arms into the back of Will's knee so that now *he* has to yell at him, *Quit it, do you want to make me drop this knife?*

Has to call to Barb, "Hon, can't you keep an eye on our big guy?"

And he regrets it at once, regrets it when he sees the cogwheel stiffness in the way she unfolds her six-three frame from the great room's leather sectional where she was drinking her second vodka tonic and laughing. Laughing with Brenda, their blonde heads tipped toward one another, Barb's hair a veil below which only the relaxed curve of her lips was visible. His regret balloons as Barb marches into the kitchen, narrowing her eyes at him. She yanks Aidan by the arm so that for a moment the boy is airborne and yowls in surprise. She shakes him and he goes limp and quiet as she says, voice low, "If you can't behave, we're gonna lock you upstairs for the rest of the evening. Is that what you want?"

It's Will whose eye she catches, though, as she spits out, *Is that what you want?* He drops his gaze back to the counter, mincing garlic, mincing rosemary.

From the living room: "C'mon here, little buddy, come sit with your uncle Ron and look at this pop-up book Uncle Tony and I brought you!"

"Oh, he's already torn half of it to shreds," Barb mutters, dragging Aidan by the elbow into the living room. "Our little destruction fiend. I'll set him up with a video in a minute."

Will wants to say, *He's already watched TV all morning.* He wants to say, *Can't you play with him for half an hour?* Outside the rain has ended and a milky afternoon sun smudges wan brightness across the beach. He wants to gaze out the window as he chops and see Barb chase their little boy across the sand, arms windmilling with joy for a change, while Aidan shrieks with laughter. He wants to say to Ron, *Take him outside and toss a beach ball.* Somewhere, families are surely doing all those things, or maybe it's a myth. He says nothing. A high-frequency thrum starts inside his chest and spreads across his throat, tightening his jaw. *Don't get angry.* He concentrates on the handle in his fist, loosens his grip to stop his hand from shaking.

"Thanksgiving is my favorite holiday," he had told his chairman when he agreed to take three extra nights on call so he could have the four-day weekend free and clear. For his family. For *this* piece of his family, anyway; he hadn't dared expect his older kids to come. Their mother considers it her right to have them on holidays, separation agreements be damned. It's been years since he left, but he is not forgiven. He never will be. For nearly a year after he had reached a decision, just the cliché of it kept him from taking action: they had been warned that the surgery training program had a greater than 100 percent divorce rate. He and Elena had laughed uncertainly the first time they had heard that statistic.

He does love Thanksgiving, though, or he always intends to. Since that year at Plymouth, each year he hopes this will be the year he gets it right. He shakes his head and flips off the gas under the cranberry sauce. He doesn't mind cooking; that's the pattern this marriage has fallen into. In the previous one, he barely knew how to boil an egg. But Barb refused to cook; Barb was busy starting her company. Now everyone makes cracks about how, as a surgeon, he's the expert on knives anyway. And he's relieved to see Barb relax with her friends: she's been so irritable. The hormones, she says.

She didn't tell him she'd invited Brenda until the last minute, and she exploded when he complained. Couldn't he see how rude it would be to make her take the couch, as if she were a teenager instead of one of Barb's dearest friends? As if she didn't matter, being single? So he had changed their reservation, found the last house with an extra room, though it has *three* extra rooms and a price tag to match. He just wants Barb happy.

And she's pissed at him anyway. Pissed that he's upset her mother. Pissed that he's dictating to her how to be a mother.

Sometimes when she comes toward him, berating him for something he's done or neglected to do, eyes on fire, he suppresses an urge to shield his head with his forearms. Of course she's never actually hit him. Would never. Embarrassing to think a grown man, a man who every day cuts into skin, past the soft yellow fat, through taut bands of muscle to repair the bodies of other people, that such a man would fear his own wife, even one who towers over him. He doesn't fear her—not exactly. But the last few weeks there's been a recurrence of the achy, sinewy sadness that entered him in the years with Elena, that strange mix of dread and yearning he thought he had left behind when he met Barb. Barb was so game to travel, so charming. With her energy and her big plans for them—or for herself. He took the rages for passion.

Just this morning, as Barb ranted about how insufferable her mother is, always criticizing everything they do, always judging, he thought of his own mother, Joan. Unbidden, up popped that image of Joan's streaked blonde hair and tightly clamped red dot of a mouth framed in the rear-view mirror of the Ford wagon as she drove off while his sister shrank alone on the sidewalk, mute with fear. He was seven and Beth was five, and she had stolen a Christmas ornament from the tree in the lobby of their elementary school. The red globe rolled out of her bag and onto the seat as they drove. Their mother must have caught the glint in the mirror. She had screeched to a halt. She had twisted toward them and clawed at Beth, who pressed herself against her seat.

"What is that? Where'd you get it?" she'd yelled, until finally his sister started to cry.

"It was so pretty and we don't have any," she whimpered.

"Because Jews don't put up trees," their mother spat, then added, "What a dimwitted child! What's wrong with you?" And when no answer came, she yelled, "Get out. I won't have a thief in my car!" Will's heart slammed against his ribs, but he couldn't speak. Their mother repeated, "Out!" And when the little girl stiffened, head bowed, but didn't move, Joan got out of the driver's seat, dragged Beth onto the sidewalk, stormed back into the car, slammed the door, and peeled away. Will felt himself pinioned to a block of ice, cold stinging like a burn. The ornament left a trail of glitter, a slug's slimy trace, along the gray upholstery.

"Mom!" he had finally gasped, and who knew how far they were by then. "Mommy, turn around!" But she had accelerated. "She didn't mean to! You can't leave her there!" he screamed. When he started sobbing, leaning toward her, she sent a backhanded slap against the side of his skull. "You wanna join her out there? You want out of this car too?" He muffled his sobs. She sighed and finally, finally, tires squealing, made a U-turn.

~

"Ma's never liked my friends," Barb said while getting dressed that morning. "Goes all Catholic on me about gay couples, too. I should never have invited her."

He thought at least they would be united in this: not allowing her mother to yell at their child.

But he's not supposed to publicly air grievances. And he's definitely not supposed to interfere when Barb's with her friends. Later she'll tell him he embarrassed her in front of Brenda: how *dare* he. His head already rings with the clipped, terse tone she'll take. It won't have mattered that he's spent half the day roasting a turkey so that its golden skin crackles against the tongue, or that he remembered to bring the day-old sourdough instead of the prepackaged crap she used to bake for stuffing. Ron and Tony may be the only ones to appreciate that he's made mashed potatoes two ways, one bowl unseasoned, just the way Aidan likes them.

Though she has her back to him now, he can tell her arms are crossed by the rigid way she stands. She is muttering to Brenda and Ron and Tony. He puts aside the knife and wipes his hands on the dish towel, intending to go drape an arm around her and apologize. But Brenda, who like him is a head shorter than Barb, goes on tiptoe to murmur into Barb's ear. He watches her set a hand lightly on Barb's arm, sees Barb's shoulders release. Her limbs loosen; she nods. His skin prickles.

Barb retrieves her highball and calls over her shoulder, "We're gonna go sit on the deck for a bit." Brenda grabs the vodka bottle and he calls out, "Barb . . . !" but at her glare Will pivots back to the oven, busying himself with basting. He will not preach. After all, how much harm can a few shots do, when she's abstained so diligently for the past two months? It's a holiday. She's not ready to tell her friends about the other one they've got on the way.

His fourth. A pulse of what—giddiness? nausea?—slits through him.

He throws back the remainder of his own vodka tonic, melted to mostly ice water. It dawns on him that Aidan has been left in the charge of Ron. The child is now perfectly still, head bowed over Ron's phone, while Ron clucks at him. He scans the rooms for Tony, who at that moment reappears from a bedroom. He's carrying a suitcase-sized gift bag decorated with an autumnal leaves-and-gourds theme.

"Look what else your uncles brought you!" Tony says, beaming.

"Honestly, guys—another present?" Will protests, but Aidan has already dropped the phone and is lunging at the bag, whooping.

"Not just one—*several* presents!" Tony says, giggling like a child, and soon shreds of orange and black tissue paper festoon the carpet and the balding men huddle with the child near the coffee table, building with Lincoln logs, feasting on turkey-shaped chocolate pops.

～

Will's mother-in-law refuses to come down even after he apologizes through her closed door. While Barb remains upstairs, trying to cajole her to dinner, Brenda mixes him a vodka tonic and says, "Don't let it get to you; Mrs. McCann has always been a little nutso." He's so grateful he could hug her but instead says, "I should've been nicer to her," hoping it'll get back to Barb. Brenda shrugs. "She doesn't care about nice. No pleasing that woman. You shoulda seen her at the basketball games, back in high school. When she bothered to come. Barb was already the star, y'know, everyone's cheering for her, but Mrs. McCann sits stone-faced in the bleachers, asks Barb later why she missed those two free throws. Why she would show up in public in such a skimpy uniform. Like Barb had a choice."

He snorts. "Mothers," he says. "Can't live with them, can't shoot 'em."

He'd had this idea that after dinner they would walk along the ocean, he and Barb and their boy, inhaling the salt air and watching the terns speed-walk into and out of the surf. Maybe hold hands through Aidan, one on each side of him, swinging him into the air. But all day she's turned away from the child, and if he's honest, it's nothing new. He sometimes wants to ask her why she had insisted on having children, why she had refused to marry him unless he agreed. She would ignite at that, of course: argue that she is nothing short of the perfect mother. She *adores* Aidan; doesn't he hear her tell him every day? Doesn't he see her stop him in his tracks when he's playing, grab him, kiss his lips, ask him, *How much do you love Mama?*

Why did *I* agree? he asks himself now, and he immediately thinks, *Oh, but Aidan is the sweetest child, I'm so lucky to have him. So blessed.* And lucky to have Barb: where would he be without her whirlwind energy, the way she devours life? Her boisterous parties with friends from all walks of life, people he would never have met otherwise. The VIP tickets she can access to almost any sporting event, the way she thinks fun is the opposite of sinful. The polar opposite of his first wife. He would still be ruminating about his first two kids, their solemn wide eyes as he explained, the silent way they ran after him to the door. When it was done and couldn't be undone.

And after all, his parents managed four. People do.

~

His mother-in-law accepts a plate in her room, so Barb spends dinner-time with her and Will spends dinnertime shuttling between the dining room and the kitchen, Aidan straddling his hip, having finished his meal in three minutes. Will refills wineglasses, replenishes half-empty platters, insists to Ron and Tony and Brenda that no, he doesn't need help, just sit, just enjoy yourselves; you are our guests.

⁓

Later Aidan tosses and cries in the bunk bed until Will carries him to their room and cups himself around the boy on the king bed.

"I wish we were home," Aidan whimpers.

"Don't you like the beach?" Will asks, stroking his damp gold hair.

"You can't even go swimming in it. You have to wear a jacket."

Will sighs. "I know. There's something so beautiful about it like this, though, so cold and spare. Don't you think?"

"What's spare?"

"Empty."

"Why is empty beautiful? It's just cold."

He shrugs in the darkness. Maybe this was a bad idea. "I just thought you and me and Mommy would be happy near the ocean for Thanksgiving. Like the Pilgrims. The Pilgrims who were brave enough to set out for a new land, hoping for freedom there, for happiness. Are you learning about the Pilgrims at preschool? Did you know the first Thanksgiving happened right near the ocean too, but up north, near where I grew up? Up at Plymouth Rock? Did I ever tell you . . ."

But Aidan's breath has gone slow and deep, and he doesn't respond. Soon, Will also dozes off.

⁓

He had grown up on the coast, so maybe that explained the draw. He had tried to persuade Elena to have a beach Thanksgiving in the early years of their marriage, even gave it a last shot that final year.

"Let's make a new tradition," he had said. "The Outer Banks in winter. The four of us: we can even order out the meal. Keep it simple." She went very quiet, as she usually did when she disagreed. She never said no—she would just stop saying anything. For almost a week, she barely talked to him. He brought it up a second time.

"So you want to be in some stranger's sterile house, alone, when the kids could be with their grandparents?" she had said. "My parents aren't getting any younger. This could be our last time all together." And as always, she thought the four-hour drive to the Outer Banks too much of a hassle: they would get stuck in traffic; there were sure to be speed traps.

She saw no problems with driving ten hours west to her parents' house in Muncie.

The night he acquiesced, his small daughter crawled into his lap and ran her fingertips across the stubble on his chin, trying to tickle him, but he brushed her hand away. He wrapped his arms around her and hugged her to him until she wriggled and complained that she couldn't breathe, and he let go. Something beneath his ribcage was splitting apart. Later, brushing his teeth, his middle felt suffused with a watery weight, like a rotting melon. He palpated his own abdomen, wondering if he was harboring a tumor, or perhaps an infection of some sort. Nothing seemed amiss. The week leading up to Thanksgiving, he was more exhausted than usual and yelled at his trainees in the hospital and his children at home. He had to force himself to eat. Meals tasted like sawdust.

That final trip out to Indiana, the trees looked increasingly gnarled and twisted as they slid past the windows, and each hour increasingly denuded of leaves. The sky deepened through a palate of grays to slate. He felt as if they were driving into permanent winter, into the end of days. He'd had two hours of sleep the night before, having operated for over six hours on a man whose liver cancer had spread more extensively than scans had led them to believe. And he had come home from work to find Elena packing in a sullen silence, because he had missed the Thanksgiving show his son's kindergarten class put on at lunchtime.

In the minivan, Elena had wedged herself between the two booster seats in the back and was trying to lead the kids in songs she taught in her preschool class. Their son was bored of it. Elena refused to let the kids watch more than one video per car ride, and they had tired of coloring. Their daughter, four at the time, complained she was carsick.

And somewhere around Dayton, just as he caught himself nodding off and a jolt of adrenaline cartwheeled into his fingertips and corrected the steering wheel, Will realized that he and Elena had not talked to one another that entire drive. He shuddered, thinking of what might have happened had he dozed. It seemed connected to the not talking, to her refusal to sit up front with him. He then tried to recall the last conversation they'd had: not one involving logistics for the kids, or planning errands, but the last *real* conversation, where they revealed some hidden thought or fear, shared something they loved. He couldn't remember. It wasn't a matter of days or even weeks: more like months. Maybe years? And then he tried to remember the last time she had touched him, or accepted his touch without turning away, and he had to pull over into the parking lot of a Piggly Wiggly because the weight in his abdomen had morphed into a snake that slid like molten lead into his throat. He thought he might vomit or explode.

"I need a Coke," he said, popping open the door.

"Me too!" the kids cried at once, and Elena said, "No, *none* of you needs a Coke," to which Will said, "You're right, *I* need a vodka tonic," and he caught the disgusted curl of her upper lip as he banged shut the minivan door. *She doesn't even like me*, he thought. By the time he was standing in front of the soda case, staring at the rows of bottles, he felt dazed, unsure how he had gotten there. He pictured Elena as she had been in college: tiny, delicate, shorter even than his petite mother, her pretty, serious brown eyes. Those sad brown eyes. He asked her out the day he got his acceptance letter to medical school, when he was feeling particularly happy and confident and he had wanted to throw a life ring into the depths of those eyes. Then over burgers he had asked her why she seemed so sad, and she had shaken her head and said she wasn't sad, just shy. Maybe a little worried, too.

"Well, let me take away the worry. I can make you feel very good," he had said, with more bravado than he felt, bolder than usual. "Happy." He had covered her hand with his. Her abrupt smile, beaming, crinkle-eyed, convinced him it was possible.

Staring at the soda bottles, he thought, *I have failed*. Sadness deep within her had hardened into moroseness over the years. Even on their honeymoon, she would startle when he came near her. She would profess headaches. When she confessed about the abuse, he had quietly suggested therapy, but she had reddened and gone wild-eyed, said the last thing she wanted to do was dwell on something so far in the past, divulge it to a stranger. So instead he tried to let her take the lead, to be patient, to not ask too much. After the kids were born, she plunged with relief into the bottomless well of their needs. Nothing he did for them or with them met her approval. When he suggested a date, just the two of them, she eyed him with alarm, as if he had suggested they watch porn.

He chose his soda and let the heavy glass door thud shut. Then he spun on his heel and opened it again, pulled out two more sodas. Who cared what she said? He could treat his kids. The leaden snake shifted.

~

When he hears their bedroom door swing open, he starts awake, thinking it's morning. Barb sits beside him on the bed and says, "Shhh," gesturing toward Aidan's sleeping form. The boy is splayed across the very middle of the bed. It's midnight. He's relieved at the tired, normal timbre of her voice.

"What have you been doing?" he asks.

Her breath washes over him, tinged with acetaldehyde, vodka.

"Just walking on the beach."

He takes her hand. "Alone?"

"With Brenda."

"You should've gotten me." She shrugs. He gingerly inches toward Aidan, making room for her, but she shakes her head. "Don't worry," she says. "Why don't you go back to sleep? I'll just crash out in the living room."

"No! You take the bed; I can sleep downstairs."

But she is already standing, already sliding her fingers out of his grasp. "There's actually multiple extra rooms, remember?" And one by one she pulls off her rings, then necklace, dropping them on the nightstand, and gathers up her moisturizing cream. She totters, steadies herself, turns to leave.

"Barb?" he says, and she pauses, lips compressed.

"What?"

He wants to say, *Are you glad we came to the beach? Are you happy here? Have I made you happy?*

"Did I ever tell you about the time my father decided to celebrate Thanksgiving at Plymouth Rock?" he says.

"Oh, for fuck's sake, Will! It's midnight," she hisses. "Do you think I wanna hear some corny old story about the Pilgrims again?"

And she's gone and he's alone with a sleeping child, the bed a raft spinning through a chasm.

∼

Later, when she is, in fact, gone for good, when she and Brenda have stopped pretending and suddenly everyone else acts like they saw it coming all along—hadn't *he* been able to *tell*, of course she wasn't *bi*—he will find himself talking to a woman at a dinner party, a friend of friends, someone he would like to get to know better but is terrified of, given his track record. It will be his first Thanksgiving without his children, the first since he put an end to the charade Barb wanted after their divorce, when he and she and the kids had gathered as if they were one happy family, and she checked her watch repeatedly and barely touched her food. She had sprinted to the door when Brenda tapped the horn, explaining they were late to another dinner. She had hastily stripped the kids of their food-stained clothes and pulled on clean, pressed clothes he hadn't seen her bring into his house. "Let's not keep Auntie Bren waiting," she had chirped as Aidan started to cry and the toddler looked around her, bewildered, mouth contorting into a howl. And Barb had repeated *Let's not keep Brenda waiting* in a different tone, and Aidan went round-eyed and silent. His sister's thumb slid into her mouth.

Talking to this new woman at the Thanksgiving without his children, he will say, "My most memorable Thanksgiving was when I was little, and my father decided to have Thanksgiving at Plymouth Rock."

To his amazement, her eyes will not glaze over with boredom, nor will she scowl as if that's the dumbest thing she's heard. She'll nod and say, "Really? What was that like?"

And it will come back, more vivid than the past twenty years. His mother, Joan, a floral scarf tied loosely around her blonde beehive, those beautiful high cheekbones accentuated by the wind, herding the three of them out of the car while his father lights a pipe. His father loitering behind them, puffing deeply and gazing at the waves. She must have been pregnant with his youngest brother then; he had forgotten. November on Cape Cod: the mercury in the low thirties, the whipping ocean wind, the anemic daylight. The empty parking lot. Joan snapping, "Are you sure we're in the right place?"

"You go find it; I'll start to set up dinner."

Will had skipped ahead, eager to find the rock. His mother yelled at him to slow down. His sister Beth followed at walking pace; she hadn't yet been diagnosed, but the strange listlessness had already set in. Was the baby walking yet by then? Did Joan have to carry her? Those details became murky.

And he will confide, in a murmur to this woman he feels warmer toward with each sentence, "My mother wanted to be an actress."

"And was she?"

He will shake his head, yearning and dread abruptly worming into his chest.

"She got pregnant with me," he'll say. "I know it sounds absurd, but I didn't know that until I was in my thirties. I never did the math: their anniversary, my birth date. She'd already died by the time I realized. My dad loved to tell the story of how they met at a summer house on Montauk, but only later did he add that she was in love with someone else, someone who'd stayed in the city that particular weekend. She was getting small parts in Off-Broadway productions then, and living in Brooklyn, trying to make her way."

"How sad," she says. He waves away the words.

"Eh!—that's how it goes. Whose life turns out the way they planned, right?"

She will burrow her gaze into his, so that he holds his breath and cannot blink. She will say, "Has that been your experience?" and then add, again, "How sad." As if that's not the only possibility. And then, instead of turning to their friend, who will have joined them, holding the Beaujolais at the ready to refill their glasses, she will say, "So how did the dinner at Plymouth Rock work out, in the end?"

He will think of his father, small for a man, affable, working late into the nights to provide for the growing family. His father saying, "Who would've ever thought I could snag such a beauty?" Only now does he realize Joan's smile at those comments could have passed for a wince. He will see her chain-smoking by herself on the cramped front porch of the house they eventually moved to, hundreds of miles away from the mecca of the theater world. Away from everyone she had ever known, because his father found work in the wilderness north of Boston. Joan ricocheting between silence and rage as she shopped, and cleaned, and cooked, and raised four children. Joan, for whose sudden smile he would clean his room without being asked, for whom he would race home on his bike with sprigs of thistle or Queen Anne's lace. Joan, who on a bad day would get out the belt.

"Joanie, I'm gonna give you a special treat this year!" his father had said. "I'm gonna take us all out to Plymouth Rock—just like the first Thanksgiving!" And in his own excitement—they had studied Plymouth Rock at school, and besides, his family hardly ever went anywhere—he had failed to attend to his mother's reaction. The jittery way she lit a cigarette in the house, which she rarely did. The way her nostrils flared.

"Okay, Eugene, and how're we gonna handle the food? Where are we gonna eat?"

"Don't you worry about that! You just cook it, and I'll take care of the rest. The kids'll help."

"We'll help! We'll help!" he had yelled. And thought of how excited she would be when he found Plymouth Rock for her and recited all he knew about why it was so important.

～

He had almost run right past it in the end—it was so small and un-impressive. A tan-gray boulder in the sand, exceptional only for the date stamped into it, protected by a ridiculous pagoda built around it so tourists could ogle and snap photos. "Here, Mom!" he shouted. "Over here! Come see!"

She did, and soon they all stood in a semicircle around the boulder, his sister panting slightly. Joan lit another cigarette and pulled up her shoulders. "Eh," she said. "Big deal." And right then, enormous feathery flakes began to sift from above.

He whooped with delight, looking into the sky at the miracle. He stuck his tongue out to catch the little stars. "Look, Mom! Look!" he cried, but she just groaned. "Great. Now it's *snowing!* Freezing *and* snow!" she snapped.

"It started to snow, and it was so cold our toes went numb," he will say to the woman beside him. "My mother said to my father, *Another brilliant idea from my genius husband.* I don't remember much beyond that. I guess we must have eaten in the car, then driven the several hours back home."

The woman will suck in a breath, a kind of reverse sigh. "Sounds pretty awful," she will say, not looking away, the corners of her eyes scrunching, brows lifting. "Trying so hard to make your mother happy. When it was not to be."

"Exactly." How can she see so quickly? "My father was always trying to make it up to my mother. Had all these big ideas, which usually backfired. He never saw how his great intentions actually just made her hard life harder. He loved her, though, even through all her rages and her silences." And he'll go mute at the abrupt understanding: that Joan never loved his father back. That she stoically bore the consequences of the mistake she had made.

Her silences, the whippings, were all preferable to the times she drove off, sometimes for hours at a stretch. He recalls the dark half-moon smudge on the curtain in his childhood living room, where he sat backward on the couch, pinching away the drape, waiting for her all those times she disappeared.

Had she loved *him*?

"We probably should go sit," the woman he is drawn to will say, and she'll brush his sleeve and the touch will jolt through him like the current from defibrillator paddles to a patient's arrested heart.

"Do you want to . . . ," he will begin, about to ask her to dinner, a dinner for just the two of them; he could talk to her forever. But as she turns and waits for the end of his sentence, as he looks at her, recalling what his friends told him—the buoyant gatherings with her and her husband, their warm home, her equanimity since his death—he'll say, "Um, do you want to sit near Thomas and Eleanor?" Her brows will lift, because, he can tell, she's good at reading people. He will want more than anything to see her again, to hear her voice and see her reaction to his touch, to believe that she is someone to whom he can reveal himself, who will eventually love him in his entirety anyway, but already he likes her deeply; already he knows it's more than he deserves. He tells himself he ought to spare her the pain.

Patternicity

They had both lost a husband before age forty, so a friend, Cat, introduced them. Both were left with young children. Both of their husbands had been cyclists. Their names even both began with *L*. With work and children, finding a time was difficult, but within a week of their first phone conversation, they were hiking the trail around the Washington Duke golf course. Efficiency was key now, Lenore explained: socializing while exercising, a perfect example.

Ludmilla said what do you do about places at the table—keep them the same, and leave his empty? Lenore said we did, but sometimes now we mix it up. I'm so lonely at night, Ludmilla said, and Lenore said yes. After a while it gets better. But. Ludmilla said no one understands. People act like it might be contagious. It's such a relief to meet *you.* And said nothing else because she had run out of breath.

Lenore gave her arm a light squeeze, made her voice gentle. You must accept all offers from friends to watch your kids. Then, plan lunch or coffee with another adult.

Ludmilla said no one has offered. Lenore blinked.

Ludmilla added, anyway the kids wouldn't let me. The kids freak out if I leave.

But maybe you and I?

Dinner?

Next week?

Your oldest could watch my two. Sitters are so expensive.

Lenore swallowed a mouthful of water. Wiped sweat from her brow. Said, I could ask. They are so busy though. School. Soccer. Science Olympiad.

She didn't say, they're finally having a good year.

Ludmilla's voice cracked. My kids are having such a hard time. They slam doors. The older sometimes won't talk to me at all. I think kids at school are avoiding them.

Lenore repeated, I'll ask. I'm sure my kids would want to help. Then she pointed out the dogwood, bursting like popcorn in the new green surrounding them. White, pink, open.

Ludmilla's gaze followed the sweep of Lenore's arm, and her eyes filled. Lenore apologized. Ludmilla shook her head, walked ahead a few paces, blew her nose. Sighed. Lenore shuffled her feet in the pine needles, waited.

Lenore's husband had died three years earlier, of lymphoma. Ludmilla's had fallen while rock climbing with friends in Colorado, five months ago. The families at Forestview Elementary had organized a meal tree, brought Lenore food several times a week for nearly a year. Ludmilla's family had moved to Durham only eleven months ago, and no one was sure whether Puerto Ricans ate lasagna, Ludmilla snorted. People said nice things the first week, they did try, but then they hung back. People are kind of reserved here in the South, aren't they?

Lenore shrugged. She had lived here nearly twenty years. People layered across her days like a quilt: The neighbor who taught her son to use a telescope. The colleague who baked her zucchini bread every December. The dad who drove her sons to soccer so she didn't have to leave work early. She worked part-time at the university, but when her husband died, her boss reclassified her position to make her eligible for benefits. And thank God for life insurance, she added.

Ludmilla winced. She was in a legal battle with her husband's insurer, who claimed his policy excluded accidents from certain high-risk activities. Who read the fine print anyway?

Lenore squeezed Ludmilla's shoulder: bones like birdwings beneath the fleece.

～

Three days later, Ludmilla called to ask about dinner, but Lenore's boys were headed to a soccer tournament and couldn't miss practice that week. Lenore sent an email after the tournament to see if Ludmilla wanted another walk or coffee. Ludmilla responded at once. She really needed a dinner out. They set a date.

But then Lenore's best friend from college surprised her for her birthday, flying into town two nights before the dinner. Lenore emailed rather than phoning because the last time they had talked, the bitterness in Ludmilla's voice lodged an ache in her chest. Ludmilla wrote back a single line: she would wait to hear about rescheduling.

Two months later, Lenore heard from Cat that Ludmilla had changed jobs, leaving her private-school teaching job for the public system, for better pay and benefits. But in the fall, she would have to move her own children into public school, having lost the private-school faculty tuition cut. She's having a hard time, Cat said. And those poor children. Lenore said she would reach out when things calmed at the start of summer.

That June, Lenore's in-laws paid for airfare so she and the boys could join them in France for a week. Her older son discovered he and his granddad shared an interest in marine animals, and together they combed the craggy beaches on the Quiberon peninsula, hunting live sea urchins and salamanders in the tidal pools.

Lenore's younger son got Rocky Mountain spotted fever soon after they returned to Durham, and she didn't glance at email or return phone calls for a week. By the time he was fully well, school was underway, work was busy, months slid by. She flushed when she saw the note she had missed from Ludmilla but told herself she would answer in a day or two, when she could muster the right response to the unhappy and slightly accusatory tone. Her friend from college had persuaded her to try online dating, so she spent hours sifting profiles and emails from strangers. Ludmilla's message drifted to the bottom of her in-box.

Just before Thanksgiving, Lenore spotted Ludmilla in the Harris Teeter. She spun her cart toward her, then noticed the sulking girl. I swear to God you are going to kill me, Ludmilla was saying, and the girl, face blank, shrugged. Ludmilla wore sweats and her hair shone with grease. She continued, If you want to get back so bad, why don't you pick up a few of the things we need? You think it's easy, doing this all by myself? The girl lifted heavy eyes in that moment and stared straight at Lenore, who froze. But Ludmilla's gaze had dropped to the scrap of yellow lined paper in her hand, and Lenore, face on fire, swung her cart one aisle over, steering to the checkout.

In December, Lenore heard that Ludmilla was moving to Philly, where her mother lived. Cat hung her head: she wished she could have done more. Lenore said, me too. Cat said, you tried. You guys recovered so well, but . . . it's like a black cloud follows that family!

Lenore phoned Ludmilla that evening, and again the next. She hung up without leaving a message. She had trouble sleeping that night, and the next, but after all, even in the days of caller ID, not everyone picks up.

Bicth

The chanterelles like rain; Casey doesn't. Rain gives his mother headaches. But the Bicth likes chanterelles, all mushrooms really, and Casey's father likes *her*, apparently more than his own sons, so here they are in a mossy cabin in the most humid county in the state, the second rainiest county in the whole *country*, so they can hunt down mushrooms.

The cabin smells of wood smoke and mold and desiccated mouse shit. At least that was what his mother suggested earlier over the phone when Casey complained of the weird dry earthy odor. They had to drive two miles up Betty's Creek Road just to pick up a signal. Four of them huddled around the Acura, in front of some middle school on a country road, just to make their calls. *Probably desiccated mouse shit*, his mother had said, and they had both laughed, and he had had to arrange his face and say "Nothing" when his dad asked, "What's so funny?" Had to punch his little brother—a hard, quick-sharp jab to the deltoid—when the fool insisted, "*Tell* me, what did Mom *say*? Why are you laughing?"

Not his fault that the smile caved on his father's face. The smile soft and inviting seconds ago. His father's quiet voice, the feathery touch of his fingers against Casey's shoulder, which Casey shrugged away. His father is so *naive*, he's heard his mother say. His father's eyes went hard with the punch. He yelled at Casey even though Casey hadn't started it, plus ten-year-old Angus is already bigger than him, taller and beefier: kid can take care of himself. And then the Bicth told his father to calm down, her voice gentle, while like an idiot she stuck her own body between his father and Casey, and said, "Why don't we all go into Clayton and try that ice cream place?"

"The *Dairy Queen*?" Casey made his voice drip sarcasm, deadened his eyes, though passing it in the car earlier, he had thought it would be nice to have one of those cones where the chocolate hardens into a shell around the soft serve.

"You shouldn't call her the Bicth, even in your head," his mother had said as she helped him pack last week, but she had giggled. She had laughed outright the first time he had said it, an experiment, inspired by the story *she'd* told *him* about a guy she had broken up with back in college, who then scrawled the slur across her dorm room whiteboard—but he'd misspelled it. "You bicth!" she'd mimicked, bringing her voice down an octave, bugging out her eyes, and Aunt Kiki said, "I remember that!" and cracked up along with her. "What a tool that guy was."

"You should probably try to like her," his mother said.

And: "If she annoys you, just pretend she doesn't exist."

And: *Who takes a twelve-year-old to a cabin in the middle of fucking nowhere, fucking Rabun Gap, no wireless, no television, just Angus for company? What does he expect him to* do? This last said to Aunt Kiki, when she probably thought Casey was out of earshot.

~

The chanterelles are butter yellow and their tops curl like the tips of the waves that used to cut across the bay at Bald Head Island, where Casey and Angus used to vacation with their parents. The Bicth points out their false gills, tipping her head toward his, holding the mushroom upside down on her palm. "See these ridges? See how they don't slot all the way through, like the gills on *this* one?"

She extends a frilly white mold for comparison.

Mold, fungus, that's all they are, his mother told him when Casey said the Bicth was a mycologist. His dad had shown him the word in the online dictionary. She's bewitched his dad into thinking she's also some kind of artist, though all she does is spray mushrooms with paint and then press them across canvas, or across glass plates that she then stamps onto watercolor paper, or sometimes she stands the mushrooms in front of objects and sprays paint around them. "Her work has been exhibited all over the country," his father told him, as if anyone cared. *Artists are dirt poor*, he overheard his mother tell Aunt Kiki. *If she thinks she's gonna get his money, she's got another think coming. I'll take him right back to court.*

～

It's raining when they go to bed that night, a steady drumming against the tin roof, and still raining in the morning. Their dad makes pancakes and bacon while the Bicth sleeps in, or maybe she's up and reading because she's always got her nose in a book. Maybe she's gone. But no, she emerges in a baggy tee and cut-off jeans all splattered with paint, a pinkish splotch right below her lip, and Casey's dad lights up like the Red Sox have just hit a triple. He says, "Did you get a lot done?" and she nods and apologizes and says he's wonderful for understanding her gallery deadline is in a week, and they kiss lightly on the lips and exchange a smile Casey has never seen before on his father's face.

Casey shoots her the withering glance his mother shoots *him* when he comes to dinner in his soccer uniform after practice. His mother would never allow such sloppiness at the table. Even Aunt Kiki knows to dress before coming down to eat, though one time when he had a stomachache and slipped into his mother's room in the middle of the night, he discovered his Mom didn't wear pajamas when Aunt Kiki slept over; in fact, neither woman wore anything. He had to ask his dad about this, because some questions gave his mom headaches and then she'd yell, but his dad closed his eyes for a moment and sighed, clamped his lips together, told him to ask his mom. Then added, "And by the way Kiki's not your aunt; you can stop calling her that now."

He thought he heard his father whispering something about this on the drive up here, when Casey had just come out of a nap. Casey knows how to go silent so adults forget he's there. But it was impossible to piece together the snatches of their conversation: *not my place to out them . . . yes I know I've been waiting years . . . never thinks of others . . . . . . not fair to them or to you . . .* (the Bicth's response).

I don't care about me; I care about them: his dad.

～

When the Bicth drops into a seat at the table, Casey spears the remaining five pancakes onto his fork and slaps them onto his plate. Angus yells, "Hey!" and his father tells him to put some back, but Casey doesn't, and then he and his father and Angus are all yelling at one another and cursing, and in the instant he locks eyes with the Bicth, he catches the flash of terror—that one unguarded second before she smiles and says she doesn't need any pancakes, she's brought along some yogurt; it's not a big deal. And also she's brought extra paper and paints and brushes if they want to try making their own paintings. They can work on the screened porch so if they make a mess, it's fine: "Just let yourselves have fun and take a risk, use your fingers if you want. I've brought extra smocks."

Angus looks at Casey for guidance, eyes bright, but Casey smirks and says they waste enough time on that art shit in school; this is vacation. His father lets it go. Instead they play cards and they watch a downloaded movie on the iPad and then there's nothing to do but wrestle. Angus is a crybaby; Casey has barely twisted his bent leg back an inch when the kid howls and their father yells, "Stop, you moron, you could really hurt him doing that!" His father used to be easygoing, until lately.

"Let's go foraging!" the Bicth says. She touches the tips of her fingers to Casey's father's forearm. Even though it's pouring out, his father smiles like she just said she knows where to find gold.

∼

The red clay is slick underfoot; water drips from the visor of his baseball cap and the rain jacket clings to his clammy skin. The woman points out wild orchids, turns over rocks to show them salamanders smaller than his pinky, says, "Look how beautiful, see the stripes?" and Angus goes to look, cries out *Wow*. Casey kicks at pebbles, then sticks, then mushrooms, surprised at how little effort it takes to decapitate them, and at this the Bicth says, "Honey, please don't do that," and he grunts, "Don't call me that." And now she's stopping every two feet, pointing out the delicate bright-orange buttons springing from the moss to the side of the trail, and the beefy yellow mushrooms beside a rotting log, and the nearly purple ones bigger than her hand. Those are dangerous, she says, as are the red-capped ones that look like the mushroom drawings in *Alice in Wonderland*. Casey has to admit: he's never known there were so many kinds of mushrooms. But then she gasps at a patch of tendrils, pink and slender, growing in a clump, saying, "Doesn't it look exactly like coral?" And he remembers the coral he saw in Belize when his mom took him snorkeling in December. He remembers the buttery leather of the first-class seat jetting there, how Kiki and his mom let him sit like a grownup on his own behind them. Angus had been sent off to his grandmother's, so it was just the three of them. *That* was a vacation, though his mom said, "Let's keep the details our little secret; we don't want to make anyone jealous." He wasn't sure if that meant don't tell Angus, or don't tell Dad, but just in case, he didn't tell anyone. Because he wants her to take him again, alone like that; *she* knows Angus is too annoying to bring places, though she says she'll take him on a trip of his own soon. Unlike the Bicth, his mother has a real job as an executive and she makes real money, though there's no need to go on to anyone about that either.

They've finally come across the frilled yellow-orange chanterelles. His dad and the Bicth pluck them by the handful: two, seven, ten. Angus has gotten into it, poking between the fallen leaves, holding up each mushroom for the Bicth's inspection. "Very good," she says, smiling, and then, "No, not that one," tossing a brighter, smaller orange one back onto the trail. Together Angus, their dad, and the Bicth fill a mesh bag. As they walk on, Casey dips down and picks up the discarded ones, slips them into his pocket.

"I'll make a delicious pasta with these tonight," she says.

"We don't eat mushrooms," Casey says, though Angus loves them.

"We'll make yours plain," his dad says.

Now she's going on about how some mushrooms are poisonous, deadly even, as if he were a moron who didn't know this basic fact. It's a trick of nature to make dangerous things mimic harmless ones, though in fact the dangerous ones are often much showier, more beautiful. More enticing. But chanterelles can't really be confused with anything else, except maybe Jack O'Lantern mushrooms. Casey mimics her, twisting his mouth and pointing like he's seen old schoolteachers do in the movies, and she flushes and Angus laughs, but it's an uncertain laugh.

Casey wonders if the mushrooms in his pocket are the deadly kind or the kind that just make you throw up a lot. If he were sure, he would slip them into the pasta for a prank. Or if he could pick who got which plate, maybe he would just slip one onto *hers*, this thin pale woman with the wisps of dark frizz around her face, who speaks in that soft, hesitant way like she knows nothing for sure, who dresses in old clothes and hiking boots. Not elegant like his mother with her blonde hair sleek as silk, who let him get his own hair streaked last month, why not; who doesn't burden their housekeeper with *her* laundry because she likes to have her own things freshly pressed at the cleaner's. She sometimes lets him choose her high heels when she's going out, though she towers over everyone, men too, even without them. His mother who is most certainly *not* a dyke like Greyson said at school so that Casey had to punch him in the face and then Casey got in trouble, because *he* was certainly not going to repeat that awful word, and Greyson with his wimpy bloody nose didn't offer it up. Casey's mother stood up for him, argued, "He must have been provoked!" At home she didn't punish him, told him, "Don't let the riffraff get to you; you're better than all of them." And why shouldn't he call Aunt Kiki *aunt* like his mother tells them to, when she's always been part of the family, from long before his parents got divorced? His mother says soon Kiki will be moving in because she lost her house and they wouldn't want her to be *homeless*, would they?

He's fallen behind on the trail, rain pummeling his back, but his father doesn't notice. His father keeps talking to the Bicth up ahead, and Angus is now skipping through the puddles, making the Bicth laugh. Casey waits, waits, the distance expanding between them, his father swallowed by a tunnel of rhododendrons. His nose itches and his eyes burn as he waits, the rain drowning out all other sounds, the leaves and flowers trembling like he is inside his jacket, glittering like tears. Now it's the Bicth who steps out of the trees, who comes back through the rhododendrons to search for him. Who knows *where* his father is by now, but *she* calls back to Casey, waits, calls ahead to the others to hold up. So he forces his heavy legs into motion, catches up, though his eyes are killing him, though his chest feels like it might explode. His father is talking to Angus and doesn't even look at him, doesn't glance up once. They all start back down the trail, his father reaching a hand back toward the Bicth, interlacing fingers, and Casey reaches blindly into his pocket, watching his arm as if it were someone else's. Sees his hand expertly transfer the mushrooms from his pocket into the mesh bag tucked over his father's arm, orange melting into orange and no one the wiser.

Small Talk

Alone with the boy, Joel Stern's mind shuffles through possibilities. The words that drop into the air between them: "Did you know that after death, you can't tell men from women because their genitals recede?"

His throat constricts and his ears fill with the gallop of his pulse.

I did not just say that. What he had intended as a friendly smile has, he's sure, twisted into a frozen grimace. *For fuck's sake, tell me I did not just say that to this nine-year-old boy.*

He can tell he has in fact said something hugely inappropriate from the pop-eyed stare of the boy, Amy's son, Adam. The boy's lip curls in disgust and his head is cocked to the side. He does not speak. Joel knows it's because there's nothing to say. He runs a cottony tongue over his dry lips and mumbles, "I—I just thought you'd know that. Your mom being a pathologist and all. Has—hasn't she taken you to the morgue?"

The boy frowns and his lip twists higher. He has Amy's dark eyes and long black lashes with the almost-white blonde hair, but the cleft in his chin and that way of looking down his nose at Joel, even though he stands a foot and a half shorter, must come from his surgeon father.

"*No*-wuh," Adam says, pulling two syllables out of the word.

"N-no?" Joel stutters. This is what happens when he attempts small talk. He had hoped children might be easier than adults, but here's a nine-year-old looking at him as if he has two heads. He should have come up with some excuse, as he had been tempted to while still in the

safety of Amy's lobby. But the thought of Amy, Amy a mere eight stories above his head, floated him into the elevator. That bobbing weight-
lessness was in his heart when her voice crackled through the intercom.

It was the boy, though, who answered the door. The boy Amy speaks
of with tenderness and worry: the boy to whom she doesn't usually
introduce her dates. Amy is taking an eternity to get ready. Perhaps her
ear is pressed to the wall that separates him and Adam from her; perhaps she's listening and weighing whether he can handle things well
enough to be worth her while. Listening and deciding *no*. Thank God
at least the girl is in the bedroom with her mother. If only the boy
would stop staring, as if he's waiting for Joel to speak again, waiting for
him to say something . . . *better*.

"Doesn't your mom ever take you to work?" Joel wheezes.

The boy snorts. "She takes me to her *office*, yeah, but not to the
morgue. The morgue would be a *creepy* place for kids."

Of course, Joel thinks, of *course*, but his throat has closed off and
he just bobbles his head in agreement like an idiot. Adam continues
to fix him with unblinking interest. What is the kid thinking? Is he
disgusted by Joel's uneven skin, pitted with the scars of adolescent
acne? Joel touches his hair; he should have gotten a haircut. The summer humidity will have turned his waviness into pure frizz: he must
look like Bozo the clown. And the damned glasses. In his scramble to
pick up the phone when Amy called him back late last night, he rolled
over onto his small-rimmed frames, and he's reduced to wearing his
old, aviator-style ones. He's sure he's not half as good-looking as the
kid's father.

Joel calculates the distance to the door: three seconds and he would
be facing the metal elevator; thirty-five minutes and he would be in
his spotless kitchen, surrounded by a decade's worth of neatly stacked
cooking magazines. In the soothing silence punctuated only by the hiss
of oil in a sauté pan, he would be able to breathe again. His computer
screen would come alive with friends.

He swallows. If he makes a break for it, he'll never be able to call
Amy again. Beads of sweat erupt along his hairline.

It's the multiple sclerosis that has given him any chance with her: her own unfounded fears that men would be put off by illness. He fears a beautiful woman like her, smarter than he, will eventually realize that he is far inferior and leave him. Yet since their first two dates, he's been unable to convince himself to let her go. The reservoir of sadness in her brown eyes. The way she laughs softly, through her nose, as if afraid to let loose a full throaty laugh. The almost unbearable sense of well-being that washed over him when she laid her hand on his arm and said, "Call me soon. Tomorrow." He would never have believed that one invitation could transform his week. When he pours the same oat squares he's eaten for a year into his breakfast bowl, they taste sweeter, crispier. In the morning, he comes awake before his alarm buzzes. He's taken to shaving daily—even when he doesn't go out. He bought aftershave.

~

He doesn't flee. He cannot flee.

And now here she is, tottering slightly on cream-colored heels and wearing a sleeveless silk sheath dress, hair twisted into a French knot at the nape of her neck. Her little girl, Ashley, bounces around her, saying, "Isn't she beautiful? I picked the earrings. Do you like the earrings?"

"The earrings rock, dude," he says to Ashley, who beams and giggles—the exact effect he had hoped for. Amy flushes. Sometimes he gets it right; studying MTV helps. His glance falls on Adam, now approaching Ashley, Adam widening his eyes at his sister to impart a secret message. They say twins have telepathy: he holds a breath. The girl seems to ignore the boy. Still, it's only a matter of time before Amy hears about the conversation he had with her son, so he might as well spill it himself, now, while he can still make a dignified exit.

He blurts out, "Hey, just so you know . . ." Her eyes slide toward him, expectant and smiling, and his heart twists as he forms words in his mind—*I said the dumbest thing to Adam just now*, or *I didn't mean to say to Adam*—and he pushes the *I* out, stuttering, just as the doorbell interrupts. Ashley sings out, "It's the sitter!" as if this were the best news in the world. The boy rolls his eyes. Joel is reduced to muteness again as there's yet another stranger to meet, more scrutiny to endure. And before he has another chance to confess, they are seated side by side in a taxi, Amy's palm resting on his thigh as if it belonged there, the city blurring past their windows.

"This is all so mysterious!" she says, tilting her face up at him and smiling. "So, were you about to give me a clue? When will you tell me where we're going? Or at least let me peek in that bag?"

He hugs the tote to his other side. He tries to match her smile but keeps imagining Adam repeating his comment to her later that night.

"Not yet. Soon; soon," he says.

~

When the taxi pulls to the curb just beyond the Fifth Avenue entrance to Central Park, Joel tells himself, *Focus*. He whips out a small spray bottle. "You'll need this," he says and spritzes insect repellant onto Amy's bare arms. She jerks away from him with a small shriek. Joel colors. He rubs at the repellant with his palms. She catches his wrist.

"No—it's fine," she says, laughing. "It's fine. It just surprised me. I wasn't—don't worry." She smiles again. "A lovely combination with my perfume. Eau de DEET. OK, tell me now—where are we going?" She claps her hands together and he flushes at the childlike excitement in her voice.

He tips the driver more generously than he can afford. His hand cupped to her elbow, he ushers her out of the cab and toward the park.

"You'll see."

"In there?" She glances at her shoes. "You might have given me some warning . . ."

"No worries, mate," he says, parroting his favorite Australian actor. Out of the bag he flourishes a pair of flip-flops, hot pink and orange striped.

"Charming," Amy says, and the uneven grin that flickers on her lips almost drives the memory of his conversation with her son from his mind. She slips on the flip-flops and hands him her heels. His thumb registers the moist warmth on the insteps—*her* warmth—as he drops them in the tote.

"We're having dinner in the park?"

He shrugs and presses his lips together. She giggles. She squeezes his hand. His spine straightens. They hold hands and follow the gravel path in.

⁓

They had been introduced a month ago, at a baby shower for his college roommate Ray, who knew Amy from medical school. Normally Joel would have sent his regrets and a nice gift, but Ray knew him too well and preempted this option. "It'll be mostly people you know," he had said, "and I've invited an amazing woman I think you'd like to meet."

Sweat sprouted in Joel's armpits. "You know I don't do setups! Or parties, for that matter!"

"You have to, man. You just *have* to expose yourself to people—to social situations—or you'll get worse and worse! And you used to be so fun. So funny." Into the silence, he added, "Plus Amy won't intimidate you. A couple of tough breaks herself recently. I really feel for her. I've told her about you and she's interested."

"You know I don't do well with first impressions. Is she a nut case?"

"She's a pathologist at New York University."

"A doctor? A doctor interested in meeting *me*—outside the office? What did you tell her?"

"I buffed the truth a little. No—c'mon, that was a joke. Joel, you've gotten way too sensitive! C'mon. I told her you were almost a chef, all right, but prefer setting your own hours. I told her you're . . . shy. She didn't blink. Don't worry. Really. She's had it with meeting other doctors. Trust me."

⁓

Joel replays the conversation he had with Adam. If he never again had to make small talk, he would be a happy man; and yet, if he could make his confession to Amy sound like small talk, that might soften it. But from their very first conversation, he and Amy have plunged into the heart of things. It's as if she reaches straight into him—as if she can't be bothered to ease into a conversation. She hums as they walk, and her hand is warm and dry in his. The blare of taxi horns, the thrum of street musicians—each noise fades as if the streets that ring the park have disappeared. A breeze strokes the leaves on the maples around them. Joel squeezes her hand and opens his mouth to speak just as Amy trips over the roots of a mulberry tree, bumps against him, and curses. He grabs her forearm and steadies her.

"I—I'm sorry," he says. "Maybe this wasn't such a good idea . . ."

"Don't be ridiculous," she says, shaking back a strand of yellow hair that's escaped its hairpins. "I should be capable of a simple walk in the park. Unless this is the start of a flare-up . . ."

Joel slaps his own forehead and says, "I didn't think of that. I *never* remember that . . ." And he turns cautious eyes toward her only to see her own eyes suddenly bright, a smile illuminating her face.

"I know," she says. "I love that about you."

The next hundred yards become a cushion of air, until Joel almost sings, "Ah—here we are!"

He gestures. Beneath the boughs of a huge sycamore sits a small, round folding table and two chairs. The table is set with a lace cloth and the china he inherited from his grandmother: nearly translucent, scalloped-edge plates limned with gold leaf. The silverware is new, purchased for this occasion, for tonight and the promise of all the other dinners he hopes to make her. A magenta peony nods its heavy head in a polished silver bud vase. Against the roots of the tree: a wicker picnic basket. Ray, wearing his newborn against his stomach in a sling, paces back and forth, back and forth, keeping guard. When he sees them, he waves, presses a finger to his lips, and points to the baby. He pantomimes sleep. They nod in silence.

"Thanks a million," Joel whispers, and Ray gives him a thumbs-up sign and blows a kiss toward Amy. She waves. Ray disappears down the path. Amy's eyes mist as she traces the edge of a plate with her finger.

"The trouble you've gone to . . . the planning . . . ," she says. "And Ray—that sneak! I talked to him just yesterday—told him we were going out so obviously he knew—but he didn't let on!"

"Men," Joel says, and she echoes, "Men!" shaking her head but grinning, eyes crinkling. He pulls out a chair for her, bowing slightly from the waist. "OK—dinner, madam, is served."

"This is—I'm just—speechless," she says. "You are so creative!"

He draws a bottle of chilled sauvignon out of an insulated compartment in his tote bag and fills Amy's wineglass.

"You don't mind that we're not in an air-conditioned room at Le
Bernardin or some other hard-to-get place?" he asks. She dismisses the
idea with a flutter of her fingers.

"I've eaten in lots of fancy New York restaurants," she says. "Every
new faculty recruit requires the latest hot restaurant. But I've never
eaten al fresco in Central Park!"

"Necessity is the mother of invention," he murmurs, sinking into
the chair across from her and filling his own wineglass to the rim.

"What?"

"Nothing. Here are the—the *amuses*. Caviar tartlets; I hope they're
still cold." He lifts the tiny appetizers from their bed of ice and arranges
them on their plates, hoping she'll taste the hours he spent perfecting
the pastry. He tingles under the burn of her steady gaze and glances
up to see her head tilted to the side in a manner reminiscent of the
way her son inspected him. Full of curiosity and—what? Revulsion? He
gulps a few mouthfuls of wine.

She puts down her glass. She cups her hand over his.

"No, really, Joel. I want to know. What did you mean, that comment
about necessity? Is it money you're worried about? Is that it? Look, I
know freelance cookbook editors probably don't make a ton of money;
I understand that and if that mattered to me, I wouldn't be here."

"It's not that," he manages. An abrupt pulse of sweat pastes his shirt
to his back. Rosiness streaks Amy's cheeks.

"I don't mean to interrogate you. It's just—if we're going to be
together—I—well, *we*, need to be honest with each other."

If we're going to be together! Joel thinks, and he places both palms
on the table to steady himself. If we're going to be together! He swallows, rubs his palms dry on his pants, and opens his mouth, ready to
tell her anything, everything. But her eyes have shifted away from his
face and she's picking at a loose thread in the tablecloth. "I know it's
early for me to demand this kind of honesty. I was never this—blunt,
before. But when you've been through one husband who could never
be honest about the small things, and who eventually—well, you know

that story." He nods, but she's not looking. He heard from Ray about how she had been left with the twins when they were barely two, right in the midst of an MS flare that gave her double vision so bad she had to hold onto furniture for balance even when she walked around her own apartment. She continues, "Anyway, it still embarrasses me. It was all such a cliché."

"Why would *you* be the one to be embarrassed? *He* was the one having the affair!"

Her face has gone red and she takes a mouthful of wine, coughs, and then squints back at Joel. "Look, I don't entirely blame him. He'd been worried from the beginning about two surgeons getting married. We both knew the hours. I was the one who insisted it was workable, that I'd pick up any slack. But then I didn't. I couldn't."

He wants to ask, *Does she miss him?* He says, "You're only human." She shrugs.

"We both thought we were superhuman for a while. And he really does miraculous things for people. Transplanting organs, saving lives— that's the stuff of miracles. But having the twins, and me getting sick . . . it was all just too much. And you're right; I'm only human."

"If he thought being with you was too much, he is crazy," Joel says. "To me, it seems being with you would be everything." His voice remains steady as he says this; his hands stay warm. She smiles; she turns to the *amuse* and cleans her plate. His breathing slows to normal. The moment of questioning has passed and he will not have to confess that he has to come up with ingenious ways of entertaining her because the idea of eating in crowded restaurants sucks the breath out of him and makes his head buzz. He can't go to big parties without drinking beforehand, either; nor does he do clubs or bars. But movies are fine, especially matinees, and he spends more time in front of his television than he would be willing to admit. Some of the cooking shows have been inspirational.

"I made us a cold lobster salad." He lifts the cover from a large plastic container and serves Amy. "With some fresh-baked bread . . . and cold cucumber soup. There's dessert too."

"Flowers! How gorgeous!"

"They're nasturtium." He sprinkles the gold and fiery-red blossoms over the surface of the soup. "I grow a small pot on my herb shelf in the kitchen. They're edible."

"When Ray told me you'd had chef training, I hoped you'd cook for me!" Amy says, leaning forward to sniff the bread.

"Ray exaggerated," Joel says, coloring. "I—I went to culinary school for six months and dropped out. But I am a good cook, and I like cooking, especially for friends and . . . well, *you.*" He drains his wineglass and she grabs his wrist.

"You don't have a problem with . . . alcohol, do you?" she murmurs.

"*Alcohol!*" And he is able to laugh. "For God's sake, no!" But here she is asking for the full story, why he dropped out of culinary school, and again they're inching toward the moment when she'll understand how isolated his life has been all the years since college. Why would a woman want any part of that? Quirky men, creative men—women like *that*— but men who can't face internship in a *restaurant*? Not a hospital, for God's sake, but a restaurant? Shyness was different; women found shyness charming. He had always been shy. Only toward the end of college did the panic start, the death-like fear that slammed the air out of his lungs whenever he spoke in class, the icicles of dread that pierced every new situation and made him pretend he valued grades over parties.

"I dropped out of cooking school 'cause I . . . I couldn't take the heat!" he says, trying to sound theatrical, mopping his forehead with his hand. She smiles but does not laugh. Nearby, a siren swells and recedes.

"It's just that I feel you're holding something back," she says. "I've been working on trusting my instincts. I've been on a lot of bad second dates over the last year, and most of them could've been avoided if I'd just believed what I felt on the bad first dates."

He swallows. "Did you think our first date was bad?"

"God no! I thought it was great! So why, you wonder, am I grilling you now?" A small frown crinkles her delicate forehead and her forlorn expression wrings his heart.

He blurts out, "Your son. Adam. I—I screwed up with him. I—I asked him if he'd been to the morgue."

She rests her chin on her fist, waiting. His heart pumps so wildly he's sure she can see it through his shirt. But she is focused on his eyes.

When Joel told Ray he was picking up Amy at her apartment, Ray had whistled. "She must be into you," he had said. "She never lets men meet her kids." The words floated Joel out of his kitchen into the markets, hunting: for the freshest lobster; for the tiniest strawberries, bursting with color and sweetness; for shortcake ingredients; for organic cream. A new outfit from a store, not mail order, which meant enduring the once-over of the sales associate and listening to his appraisals. The last three nights he had fallen asleep thinking of Amy and twice had awoken with an erection and the remnant wisp of a dream of making love. But now she wants *honesty*. He is nothing *but* honest, and it has never done him any good.

"Why would you discuss the morgue with Adam?" she asks. Her eyes are round, her forehead scrunched into tiny furrows. But she looks curious more than appalled. This gives Joel courage.

"I was nervous. I was making small talk."

～

Their first date, a quiet dinner at Ray's house with Ray and his wife, had gone extremely well. They discovered they both were passionate Giants fans and had both grown up in Far Rockaway, though they had attended different schools. She read cooking magazines to unwind after a long day at the hospital, though she subsisted mainly on takeout. He loved watching police dramas. For their second date, Joel had insisted on seeing Amy's workplace, and they had visited the morgue. Joel told her he didn't understand her embarrassment at being a pathologist, and he'd learned she had started out in surgery until the MS flared and made her clumsy in the OR. Her program director had suggested she consider a field where her stumbles didn't threaten a person's aortic artery.

It was cold in the morgue, and as she spoke, her back stiffened and her jaw tightened. The color leached from her face, and then the animation. Her voice, drained of verve, became a monotonous, echoing alto. She had always wanted to be a surgeon, she said. She had never given a second thought to her health. She had assumed she would be married while she was raising kids, too. But this is how it is, she had said, sweeping a hand toward the silent tiled room with its metal drawers. And Joel had folded her in his arms. He had said, "No, this isn't how it is, not all the time." Her thin back softened. To his surprise, she hadn't pushed him away, and after a while she had embraced him. When they emerged onto the sidewalk, the heat and light slapped them off balance and she clutched his arm. Then she had released him and very gently, very deliberately laid her fingers on his arm and said, "Call me."

⌒

"You were making small talk, and . . . ?" Amy arches an eyebrow.

"I was trying to find common ground. I asked him . . ." He swallows. "I asked if he knew—what you'd told me. I was sure he did. You know. About genitalia."

"*What?*"

"What you told me in the morgue?"

She shrugs, looking blank.

He drops his voice. "How after death you can't tell? You know, you can't tell a man and a woman apart?"

And her eyes expand and a flush sweeps across her cheeks and her hand flies up to her mouth and he thinks, *She will get up, this is it, she will know I'm a nut*, and there's a rumbling noise and the table shimmies and he realizes she is *laughing*. Her body is shaking and she is holding herself and a tear has squeezed onto her cheek.

"I—I'm not good at meeting new people . . . ," he stammers.

"Oh . . . my . . . God," she gasps, till laughing. She fans herself with her hand and takes a drink of water. "My God! You are a *nut!*"

"I—I'm sorry . . ."

"No—no—it's hilarious. Poor Adam—did he put you in your place?"

"He—well, in fact, he *did*," Joel says, surprise releasing the knot in his throat. "He let me know it was a ridiculous question."

"Adam is nine going on nineteen," Amy says, wiping her eyes. "He's a little protective of me. He doesn't remember a time when his dad lived with us, and I haven't—well, I don't introduce guys to him." She sips a spoonful of soup, then another. "This is the most amazing food I've had, Joel."

He could stand up in front of a room full of people. Sing. He could eat dinner on a stage and not pass out.

"It's the one thing I'm really good at," he says with a shrug. "I wish I were better with children."

⁓

On the phone, his mother had almost ruined his day. He had expected relief when he told her he was actually dating again, but a silence followed his description of Amy. "I don't want to sound . . . cruel, Joel," she'd said, each word following a silent eternity during which Joel's heart condensed further into a nub of fear. "But you sell yourself short. It's always been your way. To date a woman with *children, young* children, and with a major medical *condition* . . . well. Maybe it'll come to nothing; maybe I should keep my peace. But I have to say this to you because no one else will. What will you have to look forward to, Joel, if this goes well? Being a young widower? Raising another man's children?"

⁓

"How can you be good with children when you've never had any?" Amy says. "It's an acquired skill. It takes time. It takes effort."

"I thought you'd be furious," he says. Around her the light is shifting toward red and gold. Streaks of purple and orange tint the clouds.

She sighs. "I suppose years ago I might have been. When my sense of humor was vestigial."

Joel's words surge to meet hers. "I'm not put off by time or effort," he begins. When she leans across the table and kisses him, she knocks over the wine bottle but neither one stops and the cold liquid rushes off the table and seeps through his new linen trousers. Is it possible, he thinks, that his life might work out after all? The terror fills him, enveloping as the terror of death but less black. He drinks in her scent: lavender, jasmine, bug repellant. He stands abruptly, righting the wine bottle and starting to clear their plates.

"I have a problem being around people I don't know," he mutters, not looking at her. She takes the clinking china out of his trembling hands just as he's about to drop it.

"Calm down." Her voice is a balm. "Ray told me all about your social phobia."

He swallows. "My—*what?*"

"He's a physician, Joel. He said he's tried to tell you himself and you never listen. It's a medical condition. It's not that big a deal."

He sinks back into his chair.

"He just slapped a—a label on it—on *me*—and told you before you even met me?"

"He told you about my MS, didn't he?"

Joel nods. He feels naked. The purple shimmer of the sunset feathering the sky darkens his vision.

"A setup requires information, right? He thought I had a better chance of getting through to you, of helping you, than he does. Ray is a good friend."

Joel fumbles with the buttons at his throat: he needs air. He wants to tell her he is much more than *social phobia*, as she called it. Has he misread everything? Ray has been his closest friend. Was it all a different sort of plan? A terrible thought occurs to him and he feels the lobster salad threatening to rise back up. He has to know. He has to know.

"He—he set us up as—as what? As doctor and patient?"

And miraculously she laughs again, a full, throaty laugh. She shakes her head.

"As doctor and patient? I'm a *pathologist*, you nut! Are you a tissue sample?"

Slowly, one fiber at a time, his muscles release. Her laughter reaches him as if from a passing car, then closer, then right there, in his own chest, in his own throat. He is laughing too. It is beyond ludicrous that he thought and said what he said. The story of his life.

"I—I'm sorry—I sometimes say the dumbest things . . ."

"You're just human," she says, and just as he thinks, *Not superhuman, like your ex*, she adds, "And thank God not a narcissist, like my ex. Like half the guys I've dated. Plus."

He waits.

"You're funny." She licks a dot of mayonnaise from the corner of her lips. "With you I've laughed for the first time in years. It feels *good*. You are—good."

She sees him. His chest aches.

"My sitter is able to stay the night," she says. "I just have to make a call."

And he's hit by the colors in the sky: magenta and purple and the orange of California poppies against the darkening peaks of skyscrapers in the foreground. His hand quivers as he touches a lit match to the propane lantern that will illuminate their path back, but it's a new kind of tremor: a restless energy that buoys him to his feet. She helps him stack their things into the hand cart he had brought in early in the day; a car service should be waiting by the entrance. He doesn't care that no one will sample his strawberry shortcake tonight. In the morning, he can make a double batch of strawberry pancakes so she'll have enough to take back to the twins.

Muse

It is too foggy for the exercises today. She sits cross-legged before the sliding glass and watches the ballet of grasses in the wind. She presses the heels of her hands against the tingling tightening in her breasts, tries to stop the abrupt hardening. Like rapture. Like death.

Outside *Poaceae* swirl and bend and pop back upright shake off the droplets like she used to dip and sway when she was still part of the *corps*. They would stand shoulder to shoulder, arms draped over one another's backs as they practiced going soft, being water, being waves: letting the music in, letting it move them as one.

Outside, the grasses perform without practice. The tall ones trace figure eights in space, nod their firm spiked heads with each new gust. She recognizes these as timothy.

~

Timothy grew too on the road that led to her grandmother's house in Lazarea.

~

It's too foggy for the outdoor exercises but she's supposed to be in the common room by now with the other workshop artists. They announced at breakfast that they would take the exercises indoors. They would clear the dining area, warm up, stretch, begin.

~

It costs hundreds of dollars each day to be here.

He is paying hundreds each day. On top of paying the nanny.

On top of moving her and the baby into his house.

~

She never asked for any of it.

~

You can't stop rapture once it starts. The thin, warm liquid trickles over her diaphragm, then tickles the mound of belly beneath. She imagines it pooling in her navel. She squeezes her breasts like two ripe grapefruit but that makes it worse. She is a whirlpool, a cesspool. She shivers, rises. Strips. Waits until it ends then rubs rubs rubs clean with the wash-cloth. Wraps herself in the quilt and settles back before the glass.

Between these four walls, she has everything she needs: bed, table, toilet, tub. Electric kettle and a vat of tea. Sheets towels pillows quilt and heater in the wall.

And light: the flood of morning sun.

Each day, he shells out hundreds for her flood of morning sun. But not today.

~

She will not go to the practice today. If Mara or Tomás come to ask, she'll say she has the runs.

~

In Braşov, her mother, a pediatrician, earned two hundred dollars a month. Fifty of those were spent on dance lessons.

In Braşov, when she was five, she would sink into the meadow, the day opening its arms to her, and join the timothy in its mad undulations. Run spin leap drop. The swallows taught her how to glide, arms wide, then plummet, swoop. The teachers noticed, then her mother, then Doamna Krilov. Then came thunder of applause when she spun on stage in Bucharest. She was seventeen.

And then *he* noticed. In the country for a workshop, there for just a week, he noticed *her*. No one knew he was scouting. *I can make your dreams come true.*

To dance better than she ever had before: to be *seen* as a dancer. She *did* ask for that.

At nineteen, she is eighteen years, forty-eight weeks, two days older than the child.

Her mother, in Braşov, has no idea.

~

In Lazarea, her grandmother keeps a scrapbook with clippings from the papers. She shows them to anyone who stops by, though no one can read the English. They don't need to know English because it's an old story: the girl plucked from obscurity in the East, the man who saw in her a miracle. The man with his own troupe, his awards, his penthouse. In the scrapbook, he looks stern, grizzled. Bristling eyebrows plunge beneath his thinning hair. Often he extends an arm, directing.

Directing her. A firm, fatherly touch as he adjusts the angle of her wrist; a pat between the shoulder-blades to open her to the music.

In the scrapbook she is a blur, a streak of pink-brown moving light, a hummingbird. When forced to pause and pose, she's frozen in the camera's eye mid-smile as she looks up at him.

~

She's always looking up.

~

He's six foot two. In centimeters: a hundred and eighty-eight.

In dog years, four hundred and six.

In vodka, a liter per two days.

My second wife had the blues after our first, he says, pressing at her a coffee that she waves away. Trying to get her out of bed. *It passes.*

We just have to get you dancing again. Then you'll be yourself in no time.

He's generous with gifts. Calls her his muse.

~

She can't remember when or how it changed: one day his firm touch fatherly, the brilliant choreographer, and then one day in the studio, fingertips correct the tilt of her head mid-pose. Then: Can she stay behind, stay late? She thinks at last she'll get the solo. But in the dimming light, backs of knuckles graze her cheek, her throat. A light, lingering touch freezes her until it makes her sneeze. Which makes him laugh, so maybe eyes scrunched up, he couldn't see her wince.

~

If she'd learned to drink properly if she'd eaten more before if she'd realized what he wanted if she'd stayed with the others if she'd worn

something longer something heavier uglier thicker if she'd stayed in
Braşov if she had gone to college.

~

She can't remember what she said that night before it all went blank
before it all ended for her can't remember but she knows she meant to
say no say stop say please.

~

After, she *did* say please. Please I can pay to get rid of it please I'm too
young please I just want to dance but he said, *No*, he said, *Shhh*, he said,
It will be all right, he said, *I have done this before, let's keep it, it's not so hard
and this time I'm ready.* She's heard whispers he has children scattered
across the world, but he says, *I was young before, now I'm ready to be there
for* this one. *Here. For* you. *I want this.* And for the past nine months, he's
clothed fed housed her. Now he pays for this.

~

Yesterday on the mountain, they did exercises facing the sea of hills,
the waves of California oats. Mara and Tomás named the grasses. Mara
and Tomás said, *Soften your tongue soften your knees soften your eyelids*,
then back inside they twirled and leapt and dropped. She panted louder
than the rest; she crackled when she bent; she leaked. But she still could
leap.

She won't go to the exercises even if the fog clears. Yesterday over
dinner, Mara said, *You know he had no right*, murmured that word she
doesn't like to think. Said, *You have rights, you know*, said, *You don't have
to stay.* Mara born in Santa Cruz, hair like spun gold, knows the names
of every blade of grass, every lizard, warbler, rose. Mara hasn't told
anyone, not even Tomás, even though Tomás is her husband.

Mara said, *We can help you; you can bring the child.*

~

But she doesn't want to bring the child. This is what she cannot bring
herself to say: even thinking it hardens her breasts again. She won't
think of the miniature hands swimming through air, reaching for her,
mouth opening like a fish's. She doesn't want to bring the child. Horror
will drop like a blind in Mara's eyes if she asks, *Can I come with you, start
again, just me?*

How horrified her mother, grandmother, would be.

She watches the timothy cast off the wind, then bend again under its weight, and she stands. She slides open the doors, steps into the rain. The grasses part and shiver around her, blades the same here as in Lazarea but also different. Rooted into its soil, the timothy must stay put, no matter how it dances. But she is not the timothy. She tips her face skyward and lets the raindrops kiss her eyelids. The wind whips through her hair. Mara, born in Santa Cruz, said, *You don't have to stay. She* wasn't born in Santa Cruz but here she is now all the same. She tests a pirouette, barefoot, and winces as burrs assault her soles. She bends, plucks them out, tries again. Even in the rain and wind and shoeless, she can spin. Choose where to plant herself. Behind her the timothy whispers, watching her flit into her studio for her dance slippers.

Non-Native Species

"You feel so *hot!*" Les says to her in bed, recoiling. Rolling away.

"You're like a furnace! I'll be up all night!"

~

Maybe he was right that she was needy, since she had read in an online quiz that examined the stability of couples based on the way they shared a bed that those who sprawled away from one another, on their stomachs, not touching, were the ones secure enough in their bond to not need contact. Not needing was good.

She needed contact.

In bed she pressed her body against Les, nestled her cheek in the bristly hairs of his chest, drifted off to the *lub-dub lub-dub* music of him. The instantaneous way he dropped into snoring stilled her. He was a stomach sleeper too but could start the night on his back. Tolerated her head on his chest.

But not lately.

~

That fall the hillsides burned in California. Infernos raged toward the freeways, toward the redwoods, toward the shore. But they were not in California. They had moved to Seattle two springs earlier. On TV they watched the orange tongues lick at the edges of other lives.

~

"You're like a furnace!"

~

It alarms her. *Is* she burning? She touches the back of her hand to her own forehead, counts the bumping pulsebeats at her throat. Feels the chatter of her heart: like gunfire. *Too* fast?

~

That fall it had been over a year since she had bled, which she had been told was how you marked *the change*. She'd had no hot flashes, though, or nothing that she *thought* was one. It wasn't the sort of question you could slip into office conversation. Plus at work she had just started to hit her stride. Colleagues were inviting her out for drinks, or to dinner with their spouses on the weekend. Studies for which she had secured funding got lauded in the news.

She could finally navigate the route from home to work to super-market without consulting the GPS.

~

"Do you think I have a fever? Is something wrong with me?" she asks Les, knowing it is stupid, though he is a doctor, knowing he'll sigh through his nose and say, as he does, "Just go to sleep."

~

That fall the valleys burned and they were not in California but his children were. His children had remained in Bel Air, or the youngest ones had, in their mother's house perched high above a canyon far from flames. Every other Friday he flew to LAX to spend the next five days with them in the condo he had kept in Westwood for this purpose.

~

The days he is in LA, they rarely talk. She understands how much he has on his plate. She pictures him driving carpools. She pictures the bleachers at soccer, the arid dust at baseball games. Places she too has passed her afternoons, *spent* her afternoons, with her own kids.

Her kids were born and raised in LA, but she was born in Czecho-slovakia, which now no longer existed; she had been raised in Massa-chusetts. Les too had moved from New York to Minnesota to Los Angeles. Together they had longed for somewhere different.

The days he is in LA, her calls to him go to voice mail.

~

When they still both lived in LA, her own kids grown and in college, she drove his younger kids to school whenever he had work conflicts, but his kids complained. His ex complained too, echoing that the kids didn't like it, plus the canyons were tricky. The ex's boyfriend drove them regularly—but that was different. He was a native. Let the nanny drive them if you can't, his ex said. Les didn't like to argue.

~

You're so hot. He peels himself away from her, flips over. Seconds later the room fills with whistling snores.

~

In Seattle they can see a sliver of Elliott Bay from their condo living room window. She walks to her job at the Foundation, where she leads a global public health research team. Lately they've focused on protecting children from mosquito-borne illnesses and she doesn't mind when she has to stay late.

He had been the one to propose moving to Seattle, having been offered an opportunity at a successful start-up, an opportunity he had come to fear he was too old to have again. Years ago he had turned down other offers, feeling unable to move when he was thirty-five and raising kids the first time with a woman he says had stopped speaking to him, a woman who was never happy. He turned down offers when he was forty-five, new set of children, new woman, who left him not long after. He had never before felt that he could leave his kids. But the stress in his job kept rising rising like a bubble of lava, as did the stress with the kids, and the years skimmed past. *With you I feel I can do anything*, he had said. And: *Do you think I* want *to still be raising kids at my age?*

~

They've been together five years.

~

Job offers hadn't appeared for her like they had for him, though every year she secured grants, published papers, did work that helped children on the other side of the globe while she raised her own children, their father dead at forty from a stroke. Their father had had offers, too. In the silence after their kids were asleep, she and he discussed those offers, her calf draped across his thigh, his fingertips grazing the warm back of her neck. Sometimes they twirled amber Scotch in glass tumblers as they talked. They had been in fact considering a move when he.

⌒

And the years ticked on, ticked by.

⌒

She's read the odds of meeting a man after forty are lower than the odds of being hit by a car, so she's beaten some odds.

⌒

In the night, she reaches for Les. He winces.

"Your hands are like ice cubes!" he says, so she pulls them back. Presses her fingertips to her own belly to confirm.

Yes. Her hands, her feet, the tip of her nose: chilly. She apologizes, rises to slip on socks, blows on her fists. Sinks back into the memory foam. Tucks her frosty fists beneath the furnace of her thighs.

⌒

Once I knew a man, she wants to say. Once she knew a man, once she had a love, who'd say, *Cold hands warm heart.*

Who'd cup her hands within the steeple of his palms.

Who'd shift his weight in bed as she approached. Say, *There: I warmed a spot for you.*

And she would slip under the duvet onto toasty sheets.

Cold hands cold feet warm heart warm life.

⌒

Lately in the night when sleep eludes her, she rises rises until she hovers above the bed, spectral, weightless, like a child's stick figure rendering of herself. She watches the immobile solid slab of him, counts breaths, then flits out the window, cutting through the mist. Like a beam of light, she darts past the glow of the Ferris wheel over the water, past Space Needle, redwoods, Market, across state lines until hummingbird-like she hangs outside the windows in the Mission, windows behind which her daughter sleeps. She would never wake her daughter, doesn't have to. They talk almost daily; she knows her daughter learned to pull a double-espresso in the shop the other day, and has registered to take the GRE next week. Through the glass she can trace the rise and fall of her daughter's chest under the black cotton nightshirt they bought together during her most recent visit to Seattle. The window is beaded with moisture, though not far from San Francisco other fires burn. The cigarette butt, the airborne ember from a campfire; who knows why. The whole state is one giant conflagration. Everywhere, evacuations, but not here. Her daughter sleeps dreaming in the humid night; she hurtles on, eastward-bound.

~

It wasn't fire or earthquake that drove her from the state. In Massachusetts, like in Prague, she could feel the air change several times each year. For years she missed that, wanted to live somewhere cooler, but she's always been good at compromise. And LA did come to feel like home after a while. She had grown to love the dusty desert heat, the menthol breath of eucalyptus. With their multicolored skin and their dripping leaves, they had become her favorite tree, even after she had learned they were foreigners brought over as seeds by the Australians. The eucalyptus were non-natives who had become invasive. Apparently they could spontaneously combust: they had no need of ember or of spark to go aflame. Under the right (or wrong) conditions, if the sap that filled their veins grew hot enough, then just like that a tree simply exploded.

She had remained in Los Angeles through fire and earthquake but in the last few years, the roof of his car pressed heavy against the top of her skull as she rode with Les and his kids to soccer, the volume rising rising as they yelled first at one another and then, eventually, at her. She tried staying uninvolved, and she tried speaking with compassion. One afternoon she tried joking: "If I said the sky is blue you'd say no," and the older one said, "The sky is in fact colorless." And then she was screaming too, voice whipping laced with curses, and that did quiet them, but it left her trembling, her mouth abruptly dry.

She found herself saying, "Excuse me?" too many times at a Christmas office party, seated next to the wife of Les's department chair, who in a stage whisper went on and on comparing and contrasting Botox and Juvéderm treatments. No one at that dinner asked her what sort of work *she* did. After, she checked her own creased forehead in the Audi's passenger mirror as Les drove too fast around the hairpins in the canyon. She ran her fingers through her silvering hair. She wanted to say, *Slow down*, but instead she said, "Do you think I look old?"

⁓

The sky softens from ink to peach as she flits across the Atlantic, and now she's with her son, though getting there took longer. He's in London for the semester. She squints against abrupt daylight: catches him hunched near a window, framed against the spiral staircase of the LSE Library, notebooks splayed before him. They haven't spoken in a few days; she gives him space. She remembers what it was like to be twenty and on semester abroad. Yesterday, he texted that he bought his tickets home for Christmas, and can he bring his girlfriend? Is there room for his friend from Berlin too?

⁓

Before daybreak, she drops back into their bed. Her thighs have warmed her hands. She's neither burning nor icy by the time she sinks into a deep sleep.

⁓

That fall it had been half a year since she and Les made love, six months since he had reached for her, but when she asked, he said it wasn't her. Could she imagine how hard things were for *him*? Job not what he had expected, after all, plus so far from his kids. Why had no one *warned* him? Watching the news, seeing the trees ablaze, the snaking lines of cars evacuating. "You can't know what it's like."

"I'm sorry," she said. She didn't add, *I worry about them too.* "Why don't we bring them here for a while, over their school break? And more weekends?"

A hiss of impatient breath. "They have their own lives back home." His eyes like flint when he said she wouldn't understand.

⁓

There are in fact many things she does not understand.

⁓

His phone lights up, vibrates, while on TV they watch a good man turned into a drug dealer make a choice that causes a young woman to die. She tells Les go ahead, hits pause on the remote. But he flicks the call to voice mail. Hits play. He'll call his kids back later. He's not in the mood. He's had a long day.

She wants to ask, *Won't they be asleep later?* She wants to say, *Don't their voices soothe you like a balm?*

~

In LA, he used to say, *I'm too old for this shit*: the calls to school for fights; the getting up in the night to wash and rewash bed linens. When the kids tore screaming at each other through his house, the day the younger boy doused the older with the hose and the older boy retaliated by swinging the baseball bat in a whistling arc right at his brother's head, Les erupted at them, "I've had enough of you!"

Grabbed the bat that could have split a skull like a ripe cantaloupe but only grazed the cartilage of an earlobe. Grabbed the bat and slammed it to the floor.

"I've had enough of you, you idiots!"

Shhh, she had said to him, to them, reaching for a shoulder, trying to rub a back, all of them twisting away from her, the boys looking through her as if she was in fact a two-dimensional stick figure, no flesh nerve endings brimming heart.

~

Later, Les cried as she held him in the dark. Cried when she repeated to him, "You love them; you can show them other ways, better ways."

~

In LA, he had said to her, *You're the best thing that's ever happened to me.*

In LA, she had said, *Are you sure you want to move? They're very young.*

In LA, their friends said, *Wow, commuting from Seattle, that would be so hard.*

~

In Seattle, in the evenings, after silence, he says: "No one warned me. Why did no one warn me?"

And: "Who could've known?"

And: "You would have never left your kids."

"You haven't left yours," she says. "You're there for them, with them, in so many ways." But he glares at her.

~

From a colleague at work, she learns of a condition called *aphantasia*, where people can't form mental images. "I never understood what people meant when they told me to close my eyes and imagine myself floating down a river. I know what it means to float, to be on a river, but I don't see it projected behind my eyelids, like I now know most people can."

"What about the face of someone you love? Your wife or your child?"

He shakes his head.

"So what do you do when you're apart?" she asks.

"I just trust they exist," he says.

Is it easier to forget someone when you can't hold in your mind the edge of their jaw, the fringe of hair against their forehead? Does it make you more or less frantic when you're apart? She wonders if Les can form mental images, but she doesn't ask because by then, they rarely speak and it's not her most pressing question.

~

That fall her body changed, the skin loosening, speckling. Her hair went dry, then kinky. There were moments when her limbs failed her. If she practiced yoga without stretching first, her hamstrings twanged like cables.

That fall she began to picture people naked on the bus: the sinewy arms here; the broad hard back there. She shook her head when offered a seat; she preferred to sway, erect. To feel the heat of others against her hip.

~

Men go through menopause of a sort too, she read online. He was, after all, older than she was. In the mornings, she searched for the spark that used to brighten his eyes, the spark she had seen when he first spoke of going to Seattle. The ember that backlit their earlier days.

~

"Let me take you to dinner—I know the last few weeks have sucked," he said to her in mid-September. "They've sucked for me, too; the drama at home never ends. But you don't deserve it."

"You don't deserve it either," she began, but he put up a hand. "It's my mess. I made it; I have to deal with it."

When she brushed her knuckles against his forearm and said, "Why can't we deal with it all together?" he reddened, squeezed her hand for an instant, and then withdrew his arm. "You don't know how hard it is, raising another set of kids."

~

Don't be needy.

~

She's catching her breath as she crests the second hill on her way to work when a salt-and-pepper-haired man wearing a fleece pullover and black jeans passes her on the sidewalk, headed in the opposite direction. His green eyes crinkle when they connect with hers, and he nods, just once. In the puff of warmth the instant they cross paths, she pictures him naked. Feels his skin his warmth imagines the burn of his erection. Pictures melting to the sidewalk with him, the two of them fitting themselves one to the other as the crowd bustles past.

Then shame singes her skin.

~

That fall the wildfires spread no matter how much water catapulted from the helicopters. Firefighters died. Housebound people died. In the canyon in Bel Air, the nannies drove the kids to school, the mothers went to spin class, the fathers came home late. And Les's older son had finally stopped getting sent to the principal's office; the younger one no longer wet his bed.

~

But by winter Les wanted to move back. He wanted to take her back with him, stash her in his condo in the sun, the heat. *I know it didn't work there before, I know they said they hated you no matter what you tried, it's not you, they've been through so much, those poor kids. Someday we'll do all the things we really want to do, the things that matter.* She asked him,

When, and he said, *In eight years*, just eight years down the line. He knew it was a lot to ask, but that's just how it was.

~

"You want us to return to the life you kept saying you hated?" she asks, her hands tucked under her in the bed.

"You don't understand. I have no choice," he says. Time runs out and every day with each year they need him more they need him need—

"I also . . . ," she begins, then stops. Because what sort of person would put him in that position? "Can we talk about what's going on between us?" she says instead.

"It's not about us," he says. And: "Tomorrow—we can talk tomorrow."

He says, "God, do I need some sleep."

She doesn't say, *Is it about what they need or what you need?*

"I hope I can sleep," he says. "I never sleep."

And he turns over and two breaths later he is out.

~

She knows that in California, some environmentalists want to remove the eucalyptus groves, since they're not native and they're a fire hazard. She's read that eucalyptus trees explode because they thrive in heat. Everything about them is made to combust: their leaves a mat of kindling, their bark an extra skin. Their seeds bloom open in the aftermath of fire. After fire, they grow better, best. Adapted to a warming world, they have spread across the globe like phoenixes. She thinks, *They didn't ask to be brought as seeds in envelopes across the ocean.* She thinks, *Good for them that they found a place they love, where they can thrive.* She pictures herself walking the twenty blocks to work, the pillowy air, the bracing coffee. Holidays ahead with her children and their friends. When she pictures Land Rovers full of uniformed kids shoving into one another, trading curses, their parents and stepparents bidding against one another at the private-school fund-raising auctions where trinkets go for thousands of dollars, the images curl like photos tossed into a flame.

~

She is freezing she is simmering she is burning. Bursting. Afire. Her hair is tinder, her thighs logs. The fire extends hungry searching tongues. She rises red-orange blue-hot, a white asterisk of flames.

⁓

In the light of dawn, he may turn toward her: seek her out. He may be ready to talk. When he calls her name, his voice will break at the emptiness. Silence will greet him as he reaches toward absence, reaches alone toward wisps of smoke rising from cooling sheets.

Jump

Driving back from Greensboro, the ten-foot vaulting pole strapped to the roof of her car, Ellie Winters thinks, *I did not imagine this would be my life*. This thought pops up more and more these days. Beside her, Mikki is singing along to a hip-hop song on the radio, feet propped against the glove compartment, gold curls fluttering in the breeze.

"You can go more than twenty miles an hour, Mom," Mikki says.

"I'm doing fifty-five."

"The speed limit is sixty-five. It won't hurt the pole."

"I'm not worried about the pole."

"My driver's ed teacher says going too slow is as dangerous as going too fast."

Ellie's heart shimmies; Michael used to say those very words. "I don't know how you talked me into letting you take driver's ed when you still have two weeks before turning fifteen." She flicks her eyes to Mikki and catches the rosy flush of triumph on her daughter's pale cheek. "And while we're on the subject of perplexing topics, what the *heck* was I thinking when I agreed to let you jump? I had no idea the pole is so long!" What she really means to say is *I had no idea you'd catapult so high into the sky, and then sail back with nothing but a flimsy mattress to catch you*. She never says exactly what she means anymore.

Mikki lifts her left shoulder but then leans toward Ellie and with lips like moth wings drops a kiss on Ellie's right cheekbone. She resumes singing. The time for discussing whether Ellie would or would not allow pole vaulting was before she signed the permission slip: before she had put another three hundred dollars on her credit card. Her own mother, Helen, hadn't made any attempt to mask her disapproval: "Michaela is going to do *what*? But you're not going to *let* her?"

"She wants to," Ellie had said. "Michael wouldn't have wanted her growing up fearful. She's a good athlete."

Helen, a linguistics professor at McGill University, had sighed loudly into the phone, and Ellie could picture the pursed lips, the cocked eyebrow.

"There's more to life than high school sports—and bravery doesn't translate into unnecessary risks," Helen said. Then: "I can't imagine Michael would have allowed it."

"Michael would have *encouraged* it," Ellie had said, the blood washing into her cheeks. She had signed the permission slip that night. Now, watching the yellow hazard flags flutter on the ends of the pole, she's not sure that's true.

~

She unloads her daughter and the pole near the grassy high school field, and two lanky boys jog over to help. The taller one, who Mikki introduces as Jed, bumps Mikki's shoulder playfully as he hoists the pole onto his shoulder, and Ellie pauses at the look that boomerangs between boy and girl, the smile that blooms on her daughter's face. Has Mikki mentioned Jed before? She waits to catch Mikki's eye, but the teenagers turn away. Mikki tosses a casual good-bye over her shoulder.

Ellie tries to hold onto the glow of her daughter's happiness, to use it to push away the fear bubbling around the edges of her heart. She doesn't stay for practice. She needs the two hours anyway to catch up on laundry and groceries. She keeps her head down in the produce aisle at the Harris Teeter but before long hears her name; as soon as she sees her friend Cecilia beaming in her direction, she knows she won't make it through her to-do list.

Cecilia's eyes widen as she exclaims, "I was literally *about* to call you!" and she presses Ellie close. "Ever since Mikki stopped soccer, I never see you. Let's grab a cup of coffee. My treat." Cecilia ushers her toward the Starbucks behind the floral department, and before Ellie can say anything else, they're bumping knees at a small, round table, two lattes between them, their half-full carts parked at the store's threshold. It's unusual, even for Cecilia, to drop shopping in the middle of a Saturday just to talk. Like most of the women she knows, Ellie's entire social life is shoehorned into the hours in the bleachers during Mikki's various games, or the occasional cell phone conversation while in line at the checkout. *How I'd looked down on women like this when Michael and I were graduate students*, she thinks. *Women like me.*

Once Cecilia has chronicled her daughter's recent soccer achievements and repeated how all the girls miss Mikki, she gulps down half her coffee and leans forward.

"So. I've been wondering. Are you . . . seeing anyone?"

Ellie's shoulders creep toward her ears. "Ah—if you could imagine how busy I've—"

"—Just listen for a moment." Cecilia taps both palms on the table. "Please."

Ellie lifts an eyebrow, which the other woman interprets as permission to proceed. "So, our new goalie on the soccer team, sweet little girl from California? Turns out her daddy's a widower—wife died a year ago, aneurysm. He moved here to be closer to his family. So I thought . . ." She drops her eyes and sips her latte. Heat lashes through Ellie's chest. She watches her friend wait, and sighs.

"You thought since we've each lost a spouse maybe we'd be a good match?" she says.

"I only thought—well, you've been alone for so long, and you handle it so *well* . . . but he seems a little lost, a little . . . *dazed*. Doesn't always get his daughter to games on time, and doesn't talk much to the other moms. I mean *parents*. Though we did manage to get out of him that he's not *attached*." Cecilia winks and smiles. She exhales loudly. "He's a nice-looking man, Ellie, and he works over in the Research Triangle Park—some kind of software engineering company. Malcolm Albertson is his name. When I mentioned that I have a friend who has sailed through raising a daughter as a widowed parent—"

"—*Sailed through?*" Ellie stiffens.

"Well, you do *fine*! You *do*! Anyway, he perked up when he heard that. It'd help him, I bet, to hear how you do it. Can I give him your number?"

Ellie chokes on her coffee, spills some, ridiculous because she had seen that question coming the moment Cecilia began and it's no big deal. Hadn't she just been thinking *something* needs to change in her life? Cecilia darts from the table toward the condiments bar. Ellie stands too, suddenly too twitchy to stay in one place. She helps Cecilia blot away beads of coffee. Cecilia says, "I'm not trying to be pushy, honestly I'm not—you're free to say no . . ."

Ellie squeezes her arm. "No—I mean, it's OK, Cecilia. It's fine. Give the man my number."

~

Picking Mikki up from track practice a week later, Ellie finds herself calculating: the soccer team must have had at least two practices by now, giving Cecilia ample opportunity to pass along Ellie's number. Mikki, glancing at her as she slides into the passenger seat, says, "What?"

Ellie blinks and flushes. "What do you mean, what?"

"You looked like you were about to say something."

Ellie pulls into traffic. "No, nothing. How was track?"

"I might have sprained my thumb." Then, "Whoa, Mom, don't go psycho on me!" Mikki says as they roll across the rumble strip onto the shoulder. Ellie presses on the swollen pad of her daughter's palm and scrutinizes the taut red skin.

"I wonder if we should turn around and go to urgent care before it closes . . ."

"Coach said it would be fine with some ice. Can you please drive? I have a ton of homework and Jed said he'd message me at eight."

Ellie chews on her bottom lip. "Maybe I should at least call Dr. Wilson. I told you vaulting was dangerous!"

"No—I fell jumping the hurdles. *Please* drive."

Michael would say, *Don't worry so much. Kids sprain things.* Slowly, arms still tingling with adrenalin, Ellie pulls back onto the road. "I guess kids sprain things," she mumbles to Mikki. "And what's with Jed this and Jed that?"

"Mom!" Mikki sighs. "Jed's just a friend. He vaults too. He has some tips for me."

What would Michael say about Jed?

~

When they enter the house, Ellie heads straight for the answering machine, surprised when her heart accelerates at the blinking light. Surprised even more at the sinking sensation when it's only her mother's voice on the message. Maybe Cecilia hasn't even given this Malcolm guy her number yet. Why, *why* does she suddenly even care?

"Mom?" Mikki is squinting at her, hand on her hip, head tilted.

"What?" Ellie busies herself with pulling out pots and pans. Their aluminum bottoms clang against the stove.

"I asked you like two times what we're having for dinner. Is something going on?"

Her gut contracts. "No—nothing. I've got a deadline coming up for my copy for the press." Which is true, but Mikki looks unconvinced. The demands of Ellie's part-time freelance editing job don't usually make her zone out. "Go do your homework," Ellie says, and Mikki scowls but complies. Ellie's jaw tightens. Damn Cecilia. The last time Ellie waited around for a guy to call her was . . . she does the arithmetic in her head, and then steadies herself against the counter. Twenty-five years! Her daughter is almost the age she had been then.

She dated two other boys after that, and then in college she met Michael. Within a month, they were inseparable.

She shakes her head, shudders, then sets a pot of water on the stove. She tries to crimp shut the edges of her memory, but it's no use. Even as she turns on the radio, her head is full of Michael, of the confident way he would crook his arm around her neck so that her head rested in the soft crease in front of his elbow when they walked to class together. His fearless plunges into the future, first during their senior year, when he asked her to marry him so she wouldn't have to go back to Canada too soon—before they could properly decide whether or not they wanted to spend their lives together—and then a few years later, starting his own business just two years out of his MBA program. Moving forward with his plan even though his first cancerous mole was removed that September, right after he had leased space and hired his first employee. The way the doctor's mouth twitched when he said the cancer hadn't been *that* deep had been like a kick to the back of Ellie's knees. Michael told her not to worry. The doctor recommended quarterly checkups. Michael always went.

And she sees him going white that first time, at the basketball game when she was five months pregnant with Ellie, white straight to his lips, then blue, and she thought he had gotten too warm with all the bodies around them and the shouting because *she* was sweating, but he stiffened, then fell, jerking, people staring and a boy in the seat next to her starting to cry, and it seemed like a year before the paramedics—students, volunteers, too young surely to know what they were doing!—surrounded them and carried him out on a stretcher. There were several seizures after that first one, and worse things once they understood the cancer had spread to his brain, his liver, a wildfire that had jumped its plow line . . . but for some reason it's always that moment at the basketball game that she relives first, that moment that slaps the breath right out of her even now, all these years later, when anyone else would have learned to suppress it.

The metallic clattering pulls her back into the kitchen and she lifts the lid off the boiling water and dumps in the pasta. As she leans back to avoid the cloud of scalding steam, a lock of hair falls across her face and she recalls how Michael would reach over and brush her hair back, his fingers light against her brow, and her own fingers tracing the same arc melt the frozen blankness that usually paralyzes her in the wake of remembering. Her chest is full and warm. She presses garlic into the olive oil she's allowed to get too hot, and it sizzles and instantly darkens. She blinks. She scrapes it into the trash and starts over, because Mikki won't eat things that taste burnt.

She jumps when the phone rings.

~

"So how long was it before you went on a date, after?"

Malcolm asks this on the heels of an effortless conversation about teenage daughters and driver permits, just as she had relaxed into noticing his fresh-scrubbed scent and the warmth radiating from his square hand. Now a tremor cuts through her. She tips up her wineglass, heat feathering into her cheeks. She would lie, but something about the way he leans toward her in his poorly ironed button-down oxford, with the diagonal crease across the chest, instead extracts from her the truth: "Fifteen years."

He blinks. His mustache twitches. "I thought you said—I'd understood your husband died fifteen years ago."

She lifts her eyes to his and nods, once. He colors. He runs his hand over his mouth.

"I'm not advocating anyone wait that long, believe me," she blurts out, drowning out his quiet "So this is your first . . ." She continues, "If you'd asked me fifteen years ago, I wouldn't have believed it myself. It just . . . one year kinda became the next . . ." No need to mention the awkward setups, the way the occasional single man would materialize at a friend's dinner party, leaving her confused and tongue-tied. No need for him to know she had worn her wedding band until last year. She'd married Michael because she loved him and needed time to decide on her future before being forced to return to Canada, but once married, it felt like all she had ever wanted was to be with him. When that was no longer possible, there was Mikki, and Mikki needed holding and breast milk and gentle fingers brushing her forehead; Mikki needed upbeat games and doctor checkups and someone to pay the bills.

"I'm glad that you came out tonight," he says. She nods. Malcolm has a creased face and a sprinkling of white in his chestnut hair, but he's just a few years older than she. Men her age look so much older than they used to.

"Don't you—ahem. I mean, I don't—I honestly don't think I could make it that long on my own," he says. She winces at the look of despair in his eyes. "The third child was Lara's idea. And since we've moved, he's started wetting the bed again, and my older girl says I've ruined her life by making her leave her friends. But here I've got people—my parents can be in the house after school." He sniffs. "Do you think it was a mistake, moving?" His eyes pierce hers and he twitches his mustache again. They've known each other thirty minutes.

She shakes her head and says, "No."

He nods. "I couldn't stand it in that house, the furniture she'd picked and the walls she painted." He kneads his brow with thumb and fore-finger, then leans toward her. "It would've been so easy for you to move, with a newborn. Start over. Did you think about heading home to Canada?"

Ellie shrugs. Everyone used to ask. "Of course. I just wanted to fin-ish my degree—I had about a year to go when Mikki was born and Michael died. I thought a year's worth of work would only take a year." Malcolm's eyes crease and they both laugh drily. "But somehow after . . ."

They sigh in unison, which makes her smile. He holds her empty wineglass up for the waiter. She shakes her head and hinges her fin-gers over the glass's rim. The hunger in his green eyes quickens her breath. "I have to get Mikki in a little while," she says. He motions for the check.

"So did you finish your degree?"

She nods. "But I hold my department's record for the longest time to a PhD: ten years. You're considered a failure in academia if you take that long."

"But you finished in the end. That's great," he says.

"Well, you can't let life stop just because—you know. I try to raise Mikki the way Michael would have. I don't want her to hold back, to be afraid, just because she doesn't have a father. I don't want her to be like . . ." She chews her lip. "Me. I mean, I was going to be a professor, and write books . . ." And she thinks of the way one hour flows into the next, groceries becoming meals becoming trash, the trips out to the bin . . . the scatter of toys across her living room morphing into sport-ing gear and notes and books, the books suddenly Mikki's and not hers. The way two years slide by and still she's in the temporary job she took to pay a month's bills, and then it's five years and it's hard to even find appropriate interview clothes in her closet . . .

She jumps when his hand closes around hers on the table, surprised at the heat it sends shooting through her abdomen and down her thighs.

"It sucks you had to go through all that," he says, his voice low and deep. She swallows, pulse clicking in her throat. She wants to touch the sharp line of his cheekbone. She wants to feel his fingers brush her chin.

"Hey, I'm supposed to be the one comforting you. Showing you how well I've adapted," she says.

"Well, you're doing that too," he says. "Cecilia raves about your daughter."

She beams. She wonders how his lips feel. "I'm just lucky that she's such a great kid," she says, because she should say *something*, but what she's thinking is *People looking at us would think we're just a regular couple. This was how it used to be.* Then the room spins and she frees her hand from his. "I can't leave Mikki waiting too long," she says. Her head clears. "Let's do this again."

∿

He invites her to a movie and she doesn't know what to tell Mikki. She wipes her palms against her jeans when Mikki, eyes popping, says, "A date?"

"Not really. Just a movie with a friend."

But in the car afterward, Malcolm turns to her while they're still parked and before she can react, his bristly mustache brushes the tip of her nose, and then he's kissing her as if his life depends on it. She's wrapped in fire, remembering what it is like to be caressed, kissing back, thinking any second she'll combust, and when headlights sweep over them, she pushes him away and says, "Wow—it's like high school all over again, necking in the car," but he doesn't laugh, just turns the key in the ignition and says, "I don't know how you've gone as long as you have but I don't think I can last another *week*—I can probably leave the kids at my sister's on Saturday night, if you can come over then . . ." And Ellie fiddles with the radio knob as she murmurs, "Yup, I will."

∿

"How was your date?" Mikki asks, eyes on the TV as Ellie walks in from the garage. Ellie stiffens, and Mikki glances at her right then. "Aw— you're blushing! That's so cute!"

"It was a good movie. Do you have any plans for Saturday night?" Ellie asks.

"Saturday? I think a bunch of us might go to Kelly's house for a movie. Why? You wanna go out with your *boy*friend again?"

Mikki's voice is gentle, teasing, and she's smiling, but Ellie is mortified.

"He's not my boyfriend," she says. "But yes, I may have dinner with him."

~

Malcolm's house, in a brand-new development in Cary, is flanked on either side by empty lots; small red flags outline the foundations of his future neighbors. Straw covers the hard red clay of his front yard, protecting the dusting of grass seed. Pebbles wedge into her sandals as she totters across the gravel path. He opens the door before she rings the bell, and they both giggle.

"Sorry about all this . . . ," he says, sweeping a hand past the unpacked cardboard boxes pushed against the walls of the living room. "Lara was the one with a decorator's touch. I just haven't . . . but I've got the kids' rooms all set, and that's what counts, right?" She takes in the sofa, TV, the soccer ball wedged under the coffee table. The one framed painting of a log cabin in the snow. She feels as if she's missed a step, and sucks in a breath. She thrusts forward the wine bottle she almost forgot she was holding.

"Oh—let's open this right away," he says.

"It smells good in here." She trails him to the kitchen.

"Take-out Italian," he says. "I'm really good at takeout."

They drink the wine, standing beside the kitchen counter while their dinner spins in the microwave, and she feels shy. She says, "You know, I've never been both mother and wife at the same time." He cocks his head. She tucks her hair behind her ear. "I mean, I never thought I'd have to be a single mom—it wasn't what I signed up for, you know . . . I mean, seems like I was just telling my daughter the facts of life, telling her to wait and then to use protection if she's gonna—" And she stops abruptly, face burning, and drains her wine. Malcolm grins. He touches her shoulder and she takes a step toward him, and then his fingertips are releasing sparks as he brushes her neck, her throat. He runs his hands across her breasts and down her hips and the house disappears. She follows him down another hall and skirts the boxes in his bedroom while he lights candles and fumbles to dim the overhead lights. She kisses him, thinking, *I remember this*, thinking, *It's so good to feel wanted*; she had begun to fear *that* part of her died with Michael, but *no*. When her skirt drops away, between breaths she says, "You do have a condom or something, right?" and he groans and pushes away from her to rummage in his nightstand drawer, and then disappears to the bathroom. When he returns, fiddling with the foil packet, his eyes are hooded and a chill passes through Ellie's body.

"I'm sorry—it's just, this is new for me and I don't know you well and I'm trying to do it *right* . . ."

"There's been no one but Lara for years," he mumbles, "and we were both *clean*, if that's what you're worried about." Then he curses and suddenly he's hanging his head, sighing, and she realizes his erection is gone.

"I'm—sorry," she repeats. He's turned away from her and she puts her hand against his shoulder blade and squeezes. "It doesn't matter. Maybe it's too soon . . ."

His eyes flash when he turns back toward her. "It's not too damn soon for me. Is it too soon for you?" he snaps, and then squeezes shut his eyes and apologizes. Her stomach turns.

〜

Dinner is cold by the time they get to it, but Malcolm rushes to reheat it. "I'm just not used to that happening to me," he says over their risotto with mushrooms.

"It really doesn't matter."

"All this crap that's not supposed to happen. I was so looking forward to tonight—maybe I rushed things. Can we try again later?"

Be flexible, give it a chance, she tells herself.

"Of course."

But they're interrupted by a phone call just as they're finishing the bottle of wine: Malcolm's youngest is running a fever and asking for his dad.

"Damn—I'll bet he's picked up what his sister had at the beginning of the week," he says, stepping into his sneakers. He starts to wrap the leftovers even though Ellie is holding a forkful of salad. *It's OK*, she tells herself, scraping her plate into the trash. *He's a concerned father.* She opens the dishwasher to load it, but it hasn't been emptied yet. She fills the sink with soapy water and stacks everything there. *Three* kids, she thinks with a pang.

"Thanks." He kisses the back of her neck. "Can we take a rain check on this?"

"Of course."

~

But then the next week he's out of town on business, and the following weekend she decides to go to Mikki's track tournament in Pinehurst, as she had planned. On the drive out, goose bumps tighten her skin for no good reason, and her mind keeps flashing to Malcolm kissing the hollow of her neck, the backs of his fingers brushing her nipples. She lets Mikki blast the radio; rap, hip-hop, she doesn't change the station.

He calls while she's in the bleachers, and as she struggles to make out his words over the static—". . . hoping . . . maybe they'd . . . Saturday . . ."—a cheer explodes and she flushes when the woman in front of her twists around and says, "Did you see that? Mikki was fabulous!"

"Let me call you right back—you're breaking up," she says to Malcolm. She catches Mikki's glance toward the bleachers, and thrusts both thumbs up into the air, guilt like a fist beneath her ribs. So she missed Mikki's hurdles win; there's still pole vaulting. Mikki's first competitive vault.

"Save my seat—I'll be right back," she says to the woman beside her. She's so restless she would drop down from the second rung of bleachers if there weren't all these other parents around. What was Malcolm saying? Does he miss her? She's only been away three hours and already he's called; why does that fill her with energy? She sprints lightly across the freshly mowed grass on the far side of the field, eyes on her phone's display of signal bars. When they finally light up, she stops and, plugging her free ear, dials.

And it's just like high school: she's flying though he says nothing of consequence. She's telling him about the perfect green of the grass beneath her sandals, saying, "How do you suppose they do that?" and he's explaining overseeding and fertilizer in his rich, deep voice; she's nodding as if it's all fascinating, minutes ticking by, the roar from the bleachers like the background murmur of waves lapping the shore at low tide, until suddenly there's a socked-in silence. Ellie frowns, stomach clenching. She spins toward the track. Parents are standing in the bleachers and Carla White's dad, who is an orthopedic physician's assistant, springs down and jogs toward the field, where girls cluster around someone on the ground. *It's a big team—it could be anyone,* she tells herself, then sees the woman she had asked to save her seat standing and looking fixedly in her direction. Ellie's blood freezes. She snaps shut her phone. She cuts through air thick as water, running. It's a big team, anyone could have fallen, but it's Mikki writhing in agony on the blue vaulting mattress. It's Mikki clutching at her ankle while the coach swats her hands away and a teammate wrestles a baggie of ice onto Mikki's foot. When Mikki lets out an anguished "Mom!" Ellie pushes her way through the crowd and kneels by her daughter's head, smoothing her hair, whispering, "It's OK, honey, we're getting a doctor," but at first she mistakes the distant hum of ambulance sirens for her cell phone ringing again.

⌒

She doesn't turn her phone back on until Mikki is in the recovery room. The string of missed calls from Malcolm ends with one concerned message asking her to call him. Instead she calls Helen. She remains calm delivering the update on Mikki and then without warning erupts into tears.

"This is not something to cry about!" she stammers, blowing her nose in the napkin she had stuffed into her pocket after her fast-food lunch. "Mikki is fine!"

"Of course you cry when your child is hurt!"

"But she'll be fine. It's not like some life-threatening illness." Ellie hiccups, then breathes. "I wish I'd never let her vault!"

"Ellie. You're a great mother," Helen says. And again the sobs choke Ellie.

"I wasn't—I wasn't even watching—I didn't even see what happened," Ellie gasps between breaths. "I was on the phone. Flirting! With a man!"

She has to check her sobs to make sure that the rhythmic sound brushing her eardrum is indeed her mother's laughter.

"It's not funny, Mom!" she barks. "*Mom!*"

"Honey, I'm so glad!" Helen says. "I'm so glad you were flirting on the phone with a man. I'm so . . . *glad!*"

Ellie paces, fanning herself with her free hand. "I . . . think I'm losing my reception," she lies, and when Helen says, "You can't be doing all your living through Mikki," Ellie snaps shut her phone.

⁓

"You haven't mentioned that Malcolm guy in a while," Mikki says to Ellie as they sit through previews a few weeks later, waiting for a movie to start. Ellie is glad the lights are too dim for Mikki to see her flush.

"I've been too busy to see him." She keeps her voice even.

Mikki shoots her a sideways glance. "Too busy? You mean, because of me?" She nods toward her crutches, which lean against the seat in front of them.

"No . . . lots of things going on . . ."

"Good," Mikki says, turning back to her phone. "Because I wouldn't want you to use me as an excuse for anything. Y'know?"

And the lights dim further, and Ellie misses the first five minutes of the movie, turning Mikki's words over in her mind. Malcolm had called a few times in the week after Mikki's injury, but not since. *How is this supposed to work, anyway?* she wants to ask someone. Did he seriously think she could go out with him while her child was injured? *What am I supposed to feel?* Is she supposed to neglect her daughter for—what—some sex? And who has time, really, with a kid to raise? That day before Mikki's accident, the tingling, dizzying excitement over *nothing*. Not like the full, deep joy she used to feel with Michael. If she had been watching Mikki, if she had shown the universe how seriously and completely she cares for this one small girl, perhaps . . . She flinches when Mikki passes her the tub of popcorn. Mikki laughs at something on screen and Ellie forces her focus on the movie. *It would've been nice if*

Malcolm kept calling—acted like he really cared. She shifts her weight, pulling her numb foot out from under her, and her throat tightens. Thinks: *Maybe it's like when a limb falls asleep: when it's stinging with the blood rushing back through it, you suddenly remember it exists. Maybe this is what it feels like to come alive.*

~

She leaves a message for Malcolm on Saturday night. There's a message from him on her home phone the next day, and she's surprised he didn't try her cell. In the afternoon, she treats herself to a stop at the German bakery off the highway, and there's Cecilia's high-swinging ponytail in the checkout line ahead of her. Her spirits lift until she registers the familiar expression of pity the moment Cecilia sees her.

"I couldn't believe it about Mikki—what rotten luck! But I hear her ankle only needed a screw, and not a plate. How's she doing? How're you holding up?"

"She's fine—these things happen," Ellie says. "How are you? And your girls?" The words spill out too fast, filler conversation she can barely control, answers floating above her head, unheard, as she tries to pace herself for the question she really wants to ask.

"So . . . I guess I never told you how much I enjoyed meeting Malcolm," she says at last. "Great idea to introduce us. Have you seen him at soccer practice this week?"

"No, not this week," Cecilia says, handing the cashier her credit card. He must be out of town, Ellie thinks, just as Cecilia tucks her baguettes under her arm and swivels back toward her. "Of course, now that Colleen Norris is bringing his daughter, Malcolm doesn't come that often anymore."

Ellie stiffens and accompanies Cecilia toward the door.

"It's nice that they're carpooling," she says gingerly, watching Cecilia. Cecilia's eyes crinkle.

"Well, you know, don't you, that she finally got what she wanted!" she says, and Ellie swallows and struggles to neutralize the expression on her face. "The way that woman went after him! Bringing casserole dinners to practice, offering rides . . . and she's only been divorced two months! I think maybe they're in the same church, too."

Now they're behind Cecilia's Volvo in the parking lot, Ellie's legs shaky, her heart a lump of iron in her chest. Cecilia stares.

"Weren't you going to buy anything?" she asks, squinting at Ellie. Then, her face going pink, she adds, "You *did* know, didn't you, about Malcolm? You weren't . . ." The rosiness turns crimson. "I mean, you and he hadn't started *dating* or anything . . ."

Ellie forces a crooked smile. "No, no, not quite—but I didn't know that he's already—I mean, gosh, things happen quickly! Good for him," she says, and then again, with a small waggle of her chin, "Good for him."

~

The orthopedic surgeon presses his thumb against the bony part of Mikki's ankle and then gently flexes her foot.

"Any pain?"

Mikki shakes her head. A clap of thunder interrupts the rain's staccato beat against the flat roof of the clinic. The doctor maneuvers Mikki's ankle the other way and to the side. She winces. He nods.

"It's healing very nicely," he finally says.

"Can I vault next season?" Mikki asks.

Ellie snorts. The doctor turns toward her. "Vaulting is probably better for that ankle than other things she could do on it, since if she's doing it properly, she shouldn't be landing on her feet," he says.

"Yeah, it was totally my technique—I told you that, Mom!"

"I've read the statistics," Ellie says. "Lots of injuries with vaulting—"

"—Mom!"

"Well, I'll leave this up to you two," the doctor says, rising, frowning out at the rain. He looks fresh out of residency, tall, strong shouldered, surely childless.

"But now that she's had one injury, she's at increased risk, right?" Ellie says to him, narrowing her eyes, willing him to agree with her. He meets her gaze and then addresses Mikki.

"Yes, you are at increased risk," he says, and Mikki's shoulders slump. Then he slides his eyes back to Ellie, smiles, and winks. "You've done your homework, I see." She returns his smile, her body buzzing with the electricity of connection. The thunder drowns out his words and she waits, smiles, and he begins again. "OK, my wife would want me to say there *is* an increased risk of injury if it were *our* son sitting in that chair . . ."

She nods her head, surprised to feel disappointed rather than validated by his words, just as he adds, "But sometimes you just gotta get back on that horse," and then it's just her and Mikki in the cubicle of a room, Mikki lacing up her ankle brace, frowning and muttering.

"I know there are risks, Mom, but the coach and I totally understand why I landed the way I did and I know how to avoid it now. Plus the feeling when you're up there—you just can't imagine! I mean, I was just starting to get good, it was a freak accident—are you listening?"

Ellie has spent hours on the internet reading about freak accidents in pole vaulting, some of them fatal. Cold fingers rake fear through her chest at the memory of Mikki on the ground, the agony in her eyes, Ellie's own sense that she hadn't adequately protected her daughter. Michael's only child.

"Mom?"

She closes her eyes, trying to feel the moment in the air, the moment when her daughter releases the pole and hangs weightless above the world, just before the tug of gravity claims her. Instead of field and sky and vaulting pole, she sees the orthopedic surgeon's clear blue eyes, his sandy thinning hair, the boyish pit in his left cheek when he smiled. Things she hasn't noticed, or hasn't let herself notice, in a long time. And she thinks about desire, and love, and the order of things, how it can get mixed up and not go right and sometimes it's easier to just hit the snooze button than rise in the morning. But life can slide right by while you're hitting that damned snooze button. Her eyelids flutter open.

"Mom? Look, if it really upsets you *that* much, I don't need to do it," Mikki says, voice husky and quiet, and Ellie realizes her daughter has grabbed her icy hand to rub between her own warm palms.

Ellie's thoughts are tangled. She shivers, as if tiny splinters of ice are trickling through her veins. Maybe she'll ask Malcolm out for a purely platonic coffee, just for practice. It's been a while. She didn't really get to know him at all, and still, *still*, something about just being out and about again felt so *good*. She takes a breath and hears herself saying, "Not bad-looking, your orthopedic surgeon—but alas, married."

Mikki's jaw drops and she goes crimson, laughing. She says, "*Ma*-ahm!"

Ellie laughs too and adds, "I have to get out more," as she gathers her purse and the paperwork for the front desk and Mikki's bag. *I can't believe I just said that to my daughter*, she thinks, then chuckles again. Mikki, still smiling too as she walks into the hall, says, "Yeah, you *should* get out more."

"And the vaulting—I don't know. I'll talk to your coach. You really like it that much?"

Mikki claps her hands together and jumps, careful to land on her good ankle.

"Yes yes yes! I *love* it! And I'll have all summer to rest up, heal . . . yes, go talk to Coach Willis." She pauses, flushes, and adds, "He's not bad-looking either, you know, and there's never been mention of a *Mrs.* Willis!" Ellie swats her arm.

As they walk out toward the front desk, Mikki hooks her arm around Ellie's neck like Michael used to do, emphasizing her three-inch height advantage over her mother, and Ellie floats beside her daughter, beside this one lovely fragile infinitely breakable person whom she has to entrust daily to the weak forces of gravity, not to mention entropy. Whom she can adore but must release.

"Thanks for not completely forbidding me," Mikki says, taking her MP3 player from her pocket. "My friends are always saying I've got a cool mom." Ellie pauses, blinking, wondering if that's a good thing. Sighing, she says, "Well, I've always said carpe diem, right?" But Mikki's ears are plugged with her earbuds and she is bopping to her music, lips moving soundlessly. "And . . . I'm talking to myself again," Ellie murmurs, eliciting a knowing glance from the receptionist on whose desk she deposits Mikki's paperwork. As the glass doors slide open for them, the smokiness brightens: shafts of sunlight slice the heavy air outside, and Ellie fumbles for her sunscreen. Mikki squirms away as she tries to dab some on her freckled nose, then brandishes her own miniature tube.

"I've got it, see?" she says, too loudly over her music.

Ellie sighs. "Fine," she says, slipping her sunscreen back in her purse. But Mikki puts up a palm and tosses her tube to her mother. "Now you," she says, sweeping her palm back up toward the sun.

Acknowledgments

"One Way It Could Happen" first appeared in the *Portland Review*, June 2016.

"Bicth" first appeared in *Meridian*, spring 2020.

"Jump" first appeared in *Limestone*, winter 2015.

~

I am deeply grateful to a number of people who provided just what I needed when I needed it: be it feedback, letters of recommendation, words of encouragement, or simply an unflagging belief in my writing over many years. Among them I thank Shannon Ravenel, Elinor Lipman, Virginia Holman, Rich Scher, Amy Rogers, Michael Macklin, Charlotte Sussman, Kate Haake, and Gene Langston. Thank you to Dennis Lloyd and the other great folks at UW Press for their excellent stewardship of this project, working with skill and sensitivity in the midst of a pandemic!

Many of the stories in this book were started, completed, or revised during writing residencies. Eternal gratitude for the support of the Djerassi Resident Artists Program, the Virginia Center for the Creative Arts, the Hambidge Center, and the Wildacres Residency Program. Thank you to the visual artists and composers I met while there, who often helped me see new ways into my own work, and to poet Rebecca Morgan Frank, who connected me to a writing community in Boston when I moved here.

I could not have continued writing without the love and support of my family, who have been there for me every step of the way. Marius and Mioara Iarovici modeled a love of stories, books, and family, and stepped in to provide childcare and other support so I could attend residencies. Sorin Iarovici, always a generous reader and a creative artist in his own right, kept the faith with me and is the best brother I could hope for. The memory of Larry Katz's love and confidence in my work remains a buoy even after all these years. And thank you, thank you, thank you to Ariel Katz and Justin Katz for being the loving, generous, kind people you've always been. You have talked through many ideas with me, tolerated my occasional absences in the service of writing, rejoiced at the steps forward, and given me hope in the future. To Ariel Katz, writer extraordinaire, an extra thank you for reading, for notes, for commiseration. I can't wait to read your books!

DORIS IAROVICI'S first story collection, *American Dreaming and Other Stories*, won the Novello Literary Award and other publishing honors. She's a recipient of the *Crab Orchard Review*'s Jack Dyer Fiction Prize, the *Portland Review*'s Spring Fiction Prize, and a Pushcart nomination. Her essays have appeared in the *New York Times*, *The Guardian*, and elsewhere. She's been a Fellow in writing at the Djerassi Resident Artists Program, the Virginia Center for the Creative Arts, and the Hambidge Center. She works as a psychiatrist at Harvard University and lives in Boston.